#12

JUNIOR HIGH

THE REVOLT OF THE EIGHTH GRADE

JUNIOR HIGH

JUNIOR HIGH

#12

THE REVOLT OF THE EIGHTH GRADE

Kate Kenyon

SCHOLASTIC INC.
New York Toronto London Auckland Sydney

ISBN 0-590-41788-6

12 11 10 9 8 7 6 5 4 3 2 1   8 9/8 0 1 2 3/9

Printed in the U.S.A.   01

First Scholastic printing, September 1988

Chapter 1

Nora Ryan pushed her colorless, half-eaten salad to the middle of the lunch table and sighed. "Cedar Groves Junior High is the pits," she said.

Her best friend, Jennifer Mann, looked at her in surprise. "I can't believe you said that, Nora. You were so excited about being in the eighth grade and all. On the first day — remember?" The day school had started was vivid in Jennifer's mind. She had been apprehensive about entering eighth grade. Finding a fly in her Jell-O that first lunch period made her even more uncertain. Nora, on the other hand, had no reservations. "Is this going to be a fantastic year or what?" she had said, brushing aside Jennifer's concerns.

"That was then; things change," Nora said.

"There must be a reason for your feeling like this," Jennifer said.

"There are lots of reasons," Nora told her.

"Well, what we should do is list them. That way we can figure out what to do about them." Jennifer approached all problems as though they were projects. She had learned this system in her volunteer work. Her efforts for the Cedar Groves branch of Save the Whales had been particularly helpful in teaching her to find out all she could about a problem before she decided on possible solutions.

"For openers," Nora said, "take a look at this salad!"

Everyone focused on Nora's salad.

"These are important years. If we don't eat right when we're young — "

"Please, Nora," Susan Hillard interrupted. "Couldn't we eat just one lunch without one of your lectures on nutrition?"

Nora wanted to be a doctor, and she was concerned with the part nutrition played in health.

"It's not just the food," Nora continued. "It's . . . everything. Take a look at this room!"

Obediently, Tracy Douglas glanced around. Her blue eyes widened as though she were seeing the place for the first time.

Sighing, Lucy Armanson ran her hand through her Afro. "Do we have to?" she asked, but she looked, too.

The cafeteria was the worst room in the old school. Its pea-green walls were peeling, the ceiling was water-spotted, and, in places, the linoleum was worn through to the cement floor. A dismal place. Especially today with rain running down the dingy windows.

"And those boys!" Nora said. "Just look at *them*!"

Everyone turned in their chairs.

Tommy Ryder, the most conceited boy in class, dropped his chin and stared at them through narrowed brown eyes — his "leading man" pose. Beside him, Jason Anthony turned his eyelids inside out, stretched his mouth with a forefinger in each corner, and stuck out his tongue.

"Gross me out," Lucy said.

Nora turned her back on the boys. "What I'd like to know is what we ever did to deserve them."

Tracy shifted in her chair. She liked boys — even these. "They're better than nothing."

"They *are* nothing," Susan Hillard snapped.

"This whole place is boring, boring, boring," Nora said.

"With nothing to look forward to," Lucy added.

They all agreed. The next holiday was forever away. There was no major crisis demanding attention, no tangled relationships to unravel. School was all there was. Day after day of nothing but school.

"No one's even had a fight with anyone in weeks," said Susan, who liked a good argument.

"Who's got the energy?" Amy Williams asked. She was the eighth grade girls' gym star, but even she had slowed down the last few days.

Jennifer slumped forward, leaning her head on her hand, then pulled her long dark ponytail over her shoulder and twisted a lock of hair around her fingers. "I was feeling pretty good this morning, but now — "

Denise Hendrix set her tray on the table and sat down, carefully adjusting the creases of her charcoal-blue wool slacks. "What's happening?" she asked cheerfully.

"Nothing!" the others answered as one.

"This place is the pits," Nora told her.

Denise dug into her tuna casserole. "Oh, I don't know. It's not first class maybe — "

"It's *no* class," Susan interrupted.

" — but it's home," Denise finished.

The others mustered enough energy to laugh half-heartedly. Denise Hendrix had gone to school in Switzerland before coming to Cedar Groves. She and her family, the owners of Denise Cosmetics, lived in one of the town's few mansions. For her to call this dismal place home was totally outrageous.

"Really," Denise defended herself. "I like it. It feels good here. Comfortable."

"Are you sick or what?" Susan asked her.

"I'd trade this place for any of the schools you've gone to in a minute," Nora said.

Jennifer sighed. "Just imagine going to school in a place where you could look out a window and see mountains!"

"Just imagine going to school in a place where you could look out a window, period," Nora amended.

Everyone murmured sounds of agreement. Even on a clear day, the school windows of Cedar Groves made the world a gray, uninteresting place.

"After a while, one mountain gets to look pretty much like another," Denise said.

"But you could ski any time you wanted," Amy said. She wanted to be a gym teacher, and the thought of engaging in any sports thrilled her.

"We didn't have all that much time," Denise told her.

"At least the food was appetizing," Nora argued.

"The food was good," Denise conceded, "but every meal was like a special occasion or something. Madame Lamarte thought dining should be 'an experience.' We had to be dressed just right. There's no way we could've come down for lunch in jeans."

"I wouldn't mind that," Lucy said. With her high cheekbones, lustrous brown skin, and interest in fashion, she always looked as though she could be a teen model. Even when she wore ordinary jeans, they looked sharp.

"And we used china and crystal at every single meal!" Denise continued. She chuckled remembering those two years. When she first arrived here, she thought she'd never adjust. Everything was so relaxed. Now, her life in the Swiss boarding school seemed as unreal as a dream. She balled up her napkin and dropped it on her empty plate. "Madame Lamarte thought paper napkins marked the decline of civilization. Can you believe it?"

At the table behind them, Mitch Pauley launched a wadded bit of napkin through his straw.

It stung Tracy on the cheek. She let out a howl.

Nora, who had seen the whole thing, said, "Maybe Madame what's-her-name knew what she was talking about."

Glaring at Mitch, Tracy said, "I'll bet the boys there weren't all *CREEPS*!" She yelled the last word so that the boys heard.

"There were no boys there," Denise said.

Tracy looked stricken. "No boys?"

Denise shook her head. "It was a girls' school, remember? It wasn't so bad. There was a boys' school across the valley and we got together a lot."

"And you were younger," Jennifer said. Her own interest in boys hadn't really surfaced until this year.

"Your age," Denise reminded her. Because her family had traveled so much, Denise had lost time in school. She was now fourteen, a year older than the other girls in class.

"But you had Tony and his friends," Lucy said.

Tony was Denise's sixteen-year-old brother. When they lived in Switzerland, she had dated some of his friends, which made her the group's authority on boy-girl relationships.

Denise waved that away. "The point is, school is school and boys are boys no matter where you are. It's up to the person. She can make whatever she wants out of it."

Nora shook her head. "No one can make something from nothing. You have to have something to start with," she said.

The girls all turned to look at the boys again.

Tommy poked Jason.

Jason poked him back.

"They can't keep their eyes off me," Tommy said.

"They're probably trying to figure out what you are," Jason said.

"Oh, yeah?"

"Yeah!"

Tommy flicked a forkful of tuna casserole toward Jason. Cream sauce spattered the front of Mitch Pauley's letter sweater.

"Hey!" he said. "Watch it." His sweater was his most prized possession. He had won it for his work on the football team — he was captain — and the letter and other emblems as Best All-Around Athlete. He moistened his napkin with water and dabbed at the spots. They seemed to spread, and now his sweater was wet. He tossed the wet napkin at Tommy.

Tommy jumped up and knocked his chair over.

Sighing, the girls turned away.

Jason pulled a chair up to the girls' table. "Those two are showing their true colors," he said. "You're absolutely right not to pay any attention to them."

The girls ignored him.

"But don't judge the rest of us by their juvenile behavior," Jason continued. "We're not all dweebs."

Mia Stevens floated over to the table. Her purple vinyl pants squeaked when she sat down. She opened her domed black metal lunchbox and extracted a choco-bliss and a can of mousse. Looking from one sad face to another, she asked, "Who died?"

The girls returned her look without speaking.

Jason said, "They all did; they just don't know it yet." He stuck his finger in Susan's tapioca pudding.

She didn't react.

"If we were running this school . . ." Nora said.

Mia guffawed. "We tried that, remember?"

Earlier in the year, they had made a list of their complaints and taken it to the administration. As a result, they had been allowed to take over the school for a day.

"I don't even want to think about it," Denise said as she gathered her things and headed for the girls' room.

"Disaster," Jennifer said, remembering.

"Speak for yourself," Jason said. "I was a terrific principal."

That didn't even deserve a response.

"It was the rest of these" — he shot a glance toward Tommy — "*children* who messed things up."

Shaking up his soda can, Tommy advanced toward him.

Jason leaped to his feet just as Tommy aimed the can and pulled back the tab. The can hissed. Jason jumped clear. The cold, sticky liquid sprayed out, showering the girls.

Susan and Lucy shot to their feet and went for Tommy. In his backward retreat, Tommy stumbled into the next table and landed on Andy Warwick's lap. Andy bolted up, dumping Tommy on the floor and knocking over Marc Johnson's milk. Marc upended his plate on Andy's head. As the ketchup ran down the front of his tie-dyed T-shirt, Mia grabbed her mousse can and ran over to attack Marc.

"You lay off Andy, Marc Johnson!" she commanded.

Andy got between her and Marc. "I don't need you to fight my battles," he told Mia.

"I'm not fighting *your* battles," she said. "I'm protecting the shirt I made you!" She reached up and sprayed mousse on Marc's California-blond hair.

One table after another got caught up in the fracas. Seventh-graders knocked one another over in their hurried retreat.

Food and noise flew through the air like guided missiles. Luncheon monitors scurried around trying to restore order. The minute they brought one outbreak under control, another one flared up.

The girls' table was an island of calm surrounded by brush fires of rebellion. Left alone, Jennifer and Nora watched the confusion with an air of detachment.

Nora sighed heavily. "If something doesn't happen around here soon," she said, "I'll go stark, staring crazy!"

Jennifer made a face. "I think we all already have."

Chapter 2

"QUIET!" Joan Wesley shouted. The smartest girl in the class, she was standing at the front of the cafeteria staring up at the public address system speaker.

"What's her problem?" Nora wondered aloud.

"Must be an announcement," Jennifer surmised.

Joan always tuned into the PA as though it were an oracle.

"I didn't hear the ding-dong-ding." Nora referred to the chimes that preceded every announcement.

"With all this noise? Who could?" Jennifer asked.

The word *Announcement!* swept through the room. Mr. Donovan had finished his broadcast and signed off before the last hissed *Ssshhh!* died away. Then, "What'd he say?" echoed from table to table.

Joan Wesley stood on a chair. "Attention, everybody!" she said.

"Who made her Queen of the World?" Jason asked.

The girls turned on him. "Ssshhh!" they said.

"I can't hear her!" Tracy complained. "What's she saying?"

"If you'd shush," Susan said, "maybe we could all hear!"

"It's not me," Tracy objected. "It's the boys!"

Joan climbed down from the chair and started for the door. Everyone ran after her.

"Where's everybody going?" Nora asked as she and the others followed.

"Mr. Donovan's called a special assembly," Steve Crowley answered as he fell into step beside Nora and Jennifer.

"Hi, Steve," Jennifer said, smiling warmly. She, Nora, and Steve had been friends since kindergarten. Not long ago, however, Jennifer's feelings for Steve had changed. She had begun to think of him as a *boy* as well as a *friend*.

"Hi, Jen," he said returning her smile. "How're you doing?"

"Fine," Jennifer responded. "How about you?"

"Okay," he said.

"Listen, you guys," Nora said, "I hate to break up this fascinating conversation, but I'd like to know why we're going to the auditorium."

Still smiling at Jennifer, Steve said, "I told you, Nora: special assembly."

"But you didn't tell me why."

Steve shrugged. "I didn't hear the announcement. All I know is what Joan said."

Joan stood at an auditorium door, waving everyone in.

Nora stopped beside her. "What's happening?" she asked.

"Go in, Nora," Joan directed. "You're blocking traffic."

Nora stood her ground. "Why did Mr. Donovan call an assembly?"

"I don't know," Joan said. "Everyone was making so much noise I only got part of the announcement."

At Nora's elbow, Amy said, "I'll bet it's because of the boys."

Susan agreed. "Somebody probably reported them for having a food fight."

"But the whole school's here," Lucy observed as people flowed through the doors to their places. "If it was because of the boys, Mr. Donovan'd just want to see the eighth grade."

"Maybe he's going to make them an example," Jennifer suggested.

Denise floated past. "Can you believe it? Isn't it exciting?" she said.

The girls trudged down the aisle after her.

"Exciting?" Mia murmured. "I wouldn't go that far."

"At least the boys'll finally get what's coming to them," Tracy said.

"And we might miss French," Nora added hopefully. She'd gotten involved with a science experiment the night before and hadn't had time to finish her French vocabulary homework.

The girls were still getting settled when Mr. Donovan strode onto the stage to the podium in front of the faded green drapes.

"He doesn't look mad," Tracy observed.

"He's actually smiling," Lucy added.

"He should be smiling," Denise said.

Projecting her own feelings onto the principal, Susan said, "Right. He's finally getting the boys."

Denise, the only one of the group who had heard the complete announcement, looked at her questioningly.

Mr. Donovan tapped the mike to be sure it was on. Feedback screeched through the auditorium.

Behind the girls, Jason shot up. "They got me," he moaned and fell over the backs of the seats between Nora and Jennifer.

"Jason." Jennifer reprimanded him, "Grow up!"

"You're asking the impossible, Jen," Nora said.

From the podium, Mr. Donovan said, "You all know why I've called this assembly."

The girls turned and glared at the boys, who looked at each other and shrugged.

"It's not every day something like this happens," Mr. Donovan went on.

Thinking he meant the fracas in the cafeteria, Susan commented, "That's what he thinks!"

Mr. Donovan's eyes swept the auditorium, coming to rest on the center rows of seats where the eighth-graders sat.

Tracy turned in her seat. "Now you're in for it," she said to the boys.

"Cedar Groves Junior High has never before been honored in this way," the principal continued.

"He's not talking about the boys," Lucy said.

"Maybe X is coming to perform," Mia suggested. The rock group had been one of her favorites since their English teacher, Mr. Rochester, had told her she looked like Exene Cervenka.

Andy Warwick, who was sitting behind Mia, adjusted the dog collar around his neck and leaned forward. "Why would they come here, Mia?"

Mia shrugged. "They have to be somewhere. Why not here?"

"Being selected as one of five finalists from across the entire state is a great honor in itself." Mr. Donovan paused for reaction.

Everyone clapped. Someone whistled.

"Finalists? What's he talking about?" Nora asked.

"They must be picking the worst schools in the state," Jason said.

Mr. Donovan held up his hands for silence. "But we are not going to be satisfied with that!" he exclaimed. "We here at Cedar Groves Junior High are going to win the top honor!"

Everyone cheered.

"What are we cheering about?" Jennifer wanted to know.

"We're going to win the top honor!" Denise told her.

"Top honor for what?" Jennifer asked.

"The top bottom school," Jason put in.

"Spirit! That's what this is all about," Mr. Donovan said, "and Cedar Groves Junior High will be named 'Model Junior High of the Year' for the state because Cedar Groves Junior High has spirit!"

"It's a good thing it has something," Susan said.

Nora slid down in her seat. She felt as though the principal's words were directed as her. All this talk about spirit made her feel guilty. She'd done nothing but grumble about the place for days.

Behind her, Tommy said, "This place a model school? He's got to be kidding."

"He looks pretty serious to me," Mitch responded.

Making victory signs with his fingers, Mr. Donovan raised his arms over his head.

That brought the audience to its feet. People cheered and clapped and whistled and stamped their feet. The girls jumped up and down and hugged one another.

Feeling like a hypocrite, Nora got to her feet.

Jennifer yelled with excitement. "Can you believe it?!" She threw her arms around Nora. "You wanted something to happen and it has!"

"This isn't exactly what I meant." Nora dropped back into her seat.

Jennifer sat down beside her. "Aren't you excited?" she asked.

Jason poked Nora. "Yeah, Ryan," he said. "What's wrong with you? Haven't you got any school spirit?"

Nora turned on him. "*You* should talk!" she snapped. "All you *do* is complain!"

"So do you, Nora," Tracy put in. "Actually, I think you started it." It wasn't a judgment; just a fact.

Trying to think of a comeback, Nora narrowed her eyes and drew her mouth into a thin line. But there was nothing she could say. It was true, and she didn't need Tracy to remind her.

Jason smiled triumphantly. "So who am I to resist peer pressure?" he said.

"Jason," said Nora, coming up with a response at last. "Disa*peer*!"

Chapter 3

School spirit — that's all anyone talked about the rest of the afternoon. What it was exactly, who had it, who didn't, and how one got it, were the main questions on the lips of the eighth-graders.

Nora, who was determined to change her attitude, said, "Well, I know one thing for sure: People who complain all the time do not have school spirit."

"Then why're you doing it?" Tracy asked her innocently.

Nora was irritated. Tracy might have been right to criticize her earlier but not now. "I am not complaining, Tracy," she said between her teeth.

"Oh, yes, you are," Susan put in. "You're complaining about all the complaining."

"There's a difference," Nora said.

Wide-eyed, Tracy looked at Nora. "There is?"

"Yes, Tracy." Nora used her most patronizing tone. "But I wouldn't expect you to see it."

Tracy frowned.

Jennifer came to her rescue. Tracy sometimes lacked tact, but she was never mean. "Complaining is complaining, Nora," she said gently. "All Tracy means is we have to be more positive. Right, Trace?"

Tracy brightened. "Right," she said.

"That's what *I* meant," Nora explained. "We have to stop all the complaining and be more positive — even if it's impossible."

The teachers, too, asked questions about school spirit:

"Where's your school spirit?!" Mr. Geiger asked Jason when he yawned out loud during an explanation of real number coefficients.

"You call that school spirit?!" Mr. Armand asked Nora when she admitted she hadn't finished her homework. Even in French, the words made her cringe.

At the end of the day, everyone crowded around the bulletin board in the main hall for a look at the list of finalists.

Nora and Jennifer threaded their way to the front.

"Cedar Groves is at the top!" Tracy observed cheerily.

Susan groaned. "That's because it's an alphabetical listing, Tracy."

"Next week, Cedar Groves'll be the *only* name on the list," Lucy said.

"As the loser," Tommy put in.

"As the . . . winner!" The spin Lucy put on the last word prompted a chorus of cheers. Lucy faced the group and bowed.

Joan Wesley leaned close to the bulletin board. "Hubbard Woods is on the list!" she exclaimed.

Everyone groaned. Hubbard Woods Junior High definitely had a reputation for being on top.

"Have you ever been in that place?" Joan asked.

"I've gone by it," Tracy said. "It looks like a factory or something."

"That's because of all the glass," Joan told her. "It's really bright inside."

"And clean," Amy said. "I took swimming lessons there one summer. The locker room was incredible. They had hair dryers and everything."

"They have a television studio," someone said.

"And a photography workshop with

an awesome darkroom," Andy Warwick added. He belonged to the Cedar Groves Junior High Camera Club, which met in any free classroom it could get.

"So what?" Jennifer said. "Those are just . . . things. We've got something better."

Everyone looked at her as though they were daring her to prove that Cedar Groves was better than Hubbard Woods.

Jennifer shifted uneasily. She felt outnumbered and unsure. She needed reinforcement. "Isn't that right, Nora?" She glanced to her left where Nora had been standing, but her friend was gone. "Nora?"

Nora was marching toward the front door. She couldn't stand another minute of this whole business. Cedar Groves could not possibly win. Every other school on the list had more going for it. She was so depressed she walked right past Brad Hartley, who opened the door for her, without even seeing him.

Dashing to catch up to her friend, Jennifer couldn't believe her eyes. Usually, if Brad was anywhere in the area, Nora sensed it even if she couldn't see him.

"That was Brad holding the door," Jennifer said as she came up beside her friend.

"I didn't notice," Nora said. She pulled

her windbreaker close around her and hunched her shoulders against the cold, damp wind.

Jennifer turned to look back. Brad was still holding the door. "He's watching us."

"So let him watch."

Jennifer stopped dead. "Don't you like him anymore?"

Nora had fallen for Brad in shop class. She had had two dates with him since the beginning of the school year.

Nora kept moving. She shrugged.

Jennifer caught up with her. "You don't like him? I can't believe it! What happened?"

"Who said I don't like him?" Nora asked.

"You shrugged."

"That doesn't mean I don't like him."

"What does it mean?"

"It means . . . I can't think about Brad Hartley right now. There're more important things on my mind."

Jennifer considered that. "Like what?"

"This whole business about school, for one thing," Nora said.

"That's something to be happy about," Jennifer assured her.

"We don't have a chance."

Jennifer's natural optimism would not let her accept that. "We're up against some pretty tough competition," she admitted, "but even being a finalist is terrific."

Jennifer always saw the bright side. It was one of the things Nora liked about her friend. But sometimes — like today — Jennifer's cheerfulness made her feel worse.

"I suppose," Nora agreed reluctantly.

"Besides, there's nothing we can do about it one way or the other," Jennifer said. "We probably won't even have the chance to talk to the selection committee."

Nora had felt as though her dissatisfaction with school made defeat a certainty. But no one in authority had heard her complaints; the selection committee didn't even know Nora Ryan existed. Jennifer was right: None of this was their problem. She brightened. "We might not even see them. Maybe Mr. Donovan just fills out papers or something and the judges make their decision based on that."

"Right," Jennifer said. "So let's talk about something else."

"How about . . . Brad Hartley?" Nora suggested.

Jennifer laughed. "Or Steve Crowley?"

At home, Nora found her sister, Sally, in the kitchen.

Dressed in leg warmers and a leotard,

the older girl was rummaging through a kitchen cabinet. "Have you seen that candy bar I hid in here?" she asked as Nora came in.

"A dancer shouldn't eat candy," Nora said. "Actually, no one should. It messes up your blood sugar levels."

"I don't need a lecture, Nora — just my candy bar."

Nora set her book bag on the table and went to the refrigerator. "Have fruit. It's better for you." She extracted two apples from the crisper and offered Sally one.

Sighing, Sally took it. "You win." She got out the potato peeler and began scraping the apple with it.

"The peels are the most nutritious part," Nora said.

"Nora, please! I've had a hard day."

"So have I." Nora bit into her apple ferociously.

Sally chuckled. "Bad day at Cedar Groves Junior High, huh?" Now that she was attending the university, she acted as though there were no problems at the lower levels. She often told Nora to enjoy every minute before "you get into real school."

"We're up for model junior high," Nora told her.

"Really? Cedar Groves?" Sally smiled, remembering her own years there. "That's great!"

"I wouldn't start celebrating yet," Nora said.

In Jennifer's kitchen, the Manns' housekeeper Jeff Crawford said, "I think we should celebrate!" He squirted an extra dab of whipped cream on Jennifer's piece of warm apple cake.

"We haven't won yet," Jennifer reminded him.

"It's only a matter of time," Jeff said.

Jennifer smiled. Jeff always made her feel confident. As she tasted the first forkful of apple cake, she thought about how lucky they were to have him. After her mother died, there had been a string of housekeepers — all women — but none of them had worked out. They all blurred in Jennifer's memory. But she remembered in detail that first day with Jeff. Unlike the others, he hadn't tried to "make friends" with Jennifer and Eric. He had let them come to him. And he had never treated them as less than equals.

Jeff sat down next to Jennifer. "Well?" he asked. "How is it?"

"Delicious," she said. "Aren't you having any?"

"I shouldn't," he responded. "I'm supposed to be on a diet."

"But this is a celebration," Jennifer reminded him.

He sprang up. "You talked me into it."

Just then, nine-year-old Eric burst through the back door. "I'm starving!" he announced.

Jeff adjusted his LIFE IS UNCERTAIN, EAT DESSERT FIRST apron. Then he cut two pieces of cake and crowned them with whipped cream. "Think that'll hold you?"

Eric's eyes widened. "Two pieces?"

Saying, "Let's each start with one piece," Jeff shot Jennifer a sly grin.

Jennifer laughed. When Jeff shared his private jokes with her, she always felt very grown-up.

"Jeff thinks we'll win," she told Nora later on the phone. She pulled back her white chenille bedspread with her free hand and stretched out on her pink comforter.

In her own room, Nora turned down the volume on her latest Trilogy album. "I don't want to talk about it," she said. Her anxiety had resurfaced during her conversation with Sally, and it had bobbed around in her mind like a bell ringing a warning all through dinner.

"You're right," Jennifer said, misinterpreting Nora's motive. "We might jinx it." She shifted easily into the next item of business, one they discussed every night: "What are you wearing tomorrow?"

Nora glanced at her open closet. She prided herself on how well-organized it was. Still, that didn't make her nightly decision any easier. "Maybe we ought to dress up," she said.

"Why?" Jennifer had recently gone through a dress-up phase. Her grandmother, who had been visiting from England, had insisted she wear skirts to school. Jennifer had even gotten to like it. But not long after Sylvia Mann left, Jennifer fell into her old pattern. Jeans and slacks were more comfortable.

"I just thought we should look good in case the committee shows up or something."

Jennifer was confused. "What committee?"

"The judges," Nora said.

"For the model school? Those judges?"

"Who else?"

"I thought we weren't talking about that," Jennifer said.

Next morning, everybody was talking about it.

Lucy, who always seemed to know things before the others, informed everyone that, yes, the judges would be arriving; they'd spend one whole day in the school, visiting classes and interviewing students.

"When?" Nora asked.

"Monday, I think," Lucy said.

Jennifer groaned. Mondays were not the best days at Cedar Groves Junior High. After a weekend off, everyone was on "Tilt" until Tuesday. "They couldn't have picked a worse day," she said.

Jason glided up to the group on his skateboard. "Guess what," he said. "We're going to be invaded by aliens on Monday."

"If you mean the judges," Susan said, "we already know."

"Well, pardon me for living," Jason said and peeled off.

"The judges for the state model school competition will arrive on Monday morning," Mr. Mario announced during homeroom period. "Each room has an assignment for the day. Room 332 will host the visitors."

Everyone started talking at once.

Mr. Mario sighed his here-we-go-again sigh. "If there are any questions," he said, "let's ask them one at a time."

Tommy shot to his feet. "Does that mean we get out of classes?"

"No," Mr. Mario said. "It does not mean you'll get out of classes."

"Are we going to have a party for them?" Denise asked. She loved giving parties. Earlier in the year, she'd taken over the planning for the Halloween Dance.

It had been the most elaborate Cedar Groves had ever known.

"No, another room is in charge of refreshments, etcetera," Mr. Mario told her.

"But you said we're hosts," Jason put in.

Mr. Mario pointed a finger at him. "Glad to know you're listening, Mr. Anthony," he said.

"Well?" Jason persisted. "What exactly does that mean, Mr. Mario?"

"It means that some of our number will act as guides for the guests and as spokespersons for the students," Mr. Mario explained.

"I'll do it," Mitch Pauley volunteered.

"I'll help," Jason and Tommy said at the same time.

"Jennifer Mann and Nora Ryan will do it, thank you," Mr. Mario said.

Everyone glared at the two girls. Sitting across from one another, Nora and Jennifer exchanged surprised, pleased glances.

"How'd *they* get the job?" Tommy wanted to know. "I don't remember voting."

"Your memory's good, Mr. Ryder," Mr. Mario said. "But your knowledge of politics is poor. This room, in case you didn't know, is not a democracy."

Chapter 4

Nora and Jennifer ducked into the girls' room on the way to first period.

"This is so exciting!" Jennifer said once the door was securely shut behind them.

Nora squared her shoulders and took a turn around the room. "Let me show you Cedar Groves Junior High in all its glory," she said, pretending to escort the selection committee.

They both giggled.

"I wonder why Mr. Mario chose us?" Jennifer said.

Finger-combing her short brown hair, Nora looked at her friend's image in the mirror over the sinks. Jennifer's fair skin was flushed with excitement. She was tall and slim and carried herself with confidence. Only her hazel eyes gave a hint of the uncertainty she was feeling.

"I know why he chose you," Nora said. "Because you're good at things like this. You always know exactly what to say."

"I don't either," Jennifer protested. "I get so nervous, I just . . . babble."

"That isn't the way it comes out," Nora told her. "The way you move and everything — it always seems like you know exactly what you're doing." She fixed on her own image. Brown eyes. Brown hair. Short. Pretty ordinary, she thought. Easily lost in a crowd.

Jennifer could feel herself blushing. She knew Nora was not only building her up, she was also putting herself down. Whenever Nora felt unsure of herself, she started making comparisons.

"But I don't *ever* know what I'm doing," Jennifer protested.

"Nobody else knows that," Nora said, turning away from the mirror. "I think tall people seem more . . . confident. And you're a very outgoing person."

"So are you, Nora."

"Not in the same way. I mean I'm sort of . . . abrupt."

"I don't think that at all. You just don't waste words the way I do."

Nora had never thought of her directness in quite that way. Jennifer made it seem like an asset. Feeling lucky to have such a good friend, she smiled warmly.

"I feel fortunate to have you for a friend," Jennifer said.

"I was just thinking that about you!" Nora exclaimed.

They both laughed. It wasn't the first time one had voiced what the other was thinking.

Nora picked up her books from the shelf under the mirror. "I don't know why you feel that way, though. I mean, all I do is complain. That's another thing about you, Jen: You're always so positive."

"There's nothing wrong with wanting things to be better," Jennifer said. "You're just more observant than I am. I'll bet that's why Mr. Mario picked you."

Mia burst into the room. "You two cutting class?" she asked.

Jennifer and Nora exchanged horrified glances. "Did the bell ring?" they asked in unison.

"Any minute," Mia told them. She opened her lunchbox and took out a can of orange hair spray and another of gold glitter and began spraying her spiked hair.

Jennifer and Nora hurried out.

In the doorway, Nora whispered, "I sure hope the judges don't see *her* on Monday."

In the hall, Jason zoomed past on his skateboard.

"Or *him*," Jennifer added.

* * *

The two girls stayed after school to meet with Mr. Mario.

"I chose you two to host our guests, because I think you are mature enough to handle it," he told them.

Jennifer sat taller. She could almost feel herself growing right there in her desk chair. She smiled at Nora.

"What are we supposed to do, Mr. Mario?" Nora asked.

"When you come to school on Monday morning, go to the office. Mr. Donovan will introduce you to the committee."

"Then what?" Jennifer asked. She hoped he didn't hear the nervousness in her voice.

Mr. Mario sighed. "Then what," he repeated. "I wish I could predict that."

The girls knew what he meant. The eighth grade was an unpredictable class.

"Do we take them on a tour of the school or what?" Nora pressed.

"The details haven't been worked out yet," Mr. Mario said, "but I assume they'll go with you to your classes." He shrugged. "I'm sure Mr. Donovan will have a schedule for you Monday morning."

"May we ask people to help?" Nora wanted to know.

Mr. Mario chuckled. "I rather imagine you'll need all the help you can get. But two escorts should be sufficient. We don't want to overwhelm the judges."

"There might be something else we need help with, though," Nora said.

Mr. Mario nodded. "Yes, I'm sure there will be." He stood up. "I know I can depend on you. Just be sure to check with me before doing anything too . . . drastic."

"What should we do between now and Monday?" Jennifer asked.

Mr. Mario rolled his eyes. "Hope for the best."

By the time the girls got to their lockers, everyone had gone.

"Want to come to my house?" Nora asked as she checked her assignment book against the books in her locker.

"Can't. I'm due at the retirement home," Jennifer told her. She spent time helping out there on a regular basis.

"Couldn't you go another day?" Nora asked, knowing the answer. Jennifer was conscientious about her projects.

Jennifer closed her locker door. "There's the birthday party for all the people who were born this month."

"We should start planning for Monday," Nora said.

Jennifer smoothed a loose corner of the Save the Whales poster on her locker door. "Why don't you come over later? I should be home after five. That'll give us some time."

Nora agreed. They never ate dinner before six-thirty. Her mother was a lawyer with Legal Aid and usually came home last, rarely arriving before six. "I'll set the table and everything and then I'll be over."

As they went through the side doors, Nora said, "I wish Mr. Mario'd been more specific about what we're supposed to do."

"I think it's great he's left the details to us," Jennifer said. "He trusts us to do things the right way."

"But where do we start?" Nora wondered. "Hubbard Woods is so perfect."

"We've got a few days," Jennifer reminded her. "By Monday, Cedar Groves'll be perfect, too."

Nora laughed. "Did I say you were positive?" she teased. "I should have said ridiculous!"

Jennifer caught up with Nora at the corner of the Manns' block.

"Perfect timing!" she said.

"How was the birthday party?" Nora asked.

"It was great! It gave me some ideas about Monday."

"Like what?"

"There were banners all over: Happy Birthday, stuff like that. We could put some up, too." Jennifer stretched out her arms. " 'Welcome To Cedar Groves Junior

High.' " She turned toward Nora. "What do you think? We could ask some of the kids to make them and — "

" — hang them in the cafeteria!" Nora interrupted. "That way we could cover up some of the peeling paint."

"I was thinking of putting them in the main hall," Jennifer said.

"We can hang them there, too," Nora assured her. "There're all sorts of places we can put them." She laughed. "Maybe we should drape the whole school in one giant banner!"

Jennifer giggled. "We'll put the word 'perfect' on it."

"On *all* of them!" Nora amended. " 'Welcome to Cedar Groves, The *Perfect* Junior High.' If we say it enough, maybe the judges'll believe it!"

Laughing, they went to Jen's house.

At the kitchen table, Jeff stopped sorting laundry. "Judging by your happy faces, I'd say school must be a wonderful place these days," he said.

"Perfect!" the girls responded.

Jeff's round face lit up. "You won!"

"The judges aren't coming till Monday," Jennifer told him.

"And Jen and I are going to show them around," Nora added. "We're like class representatives or something."

"Whoever chose you has good taste," Jeff said. He handed Jennifer the socks to sort. "You'll win for sure."

Jennifer passed half the socks to Nora. "The competition's tough," she said.

"We have to figure out what we can do to make the place look . . . better," Nora told him.

"And the people!" Jennifer put in. "If the judges see Jason in the halls on that stupid skateboard. . . ."

"Or Mia and Andy! One look, and the judges'll probably faint!"

Jeff laughed. "Don't expect perfection."

"Why not?" Nora asked. "Hubbard Woods is perfect."

"The school is always better on the other side of the fence," Jeff paraphrased. "Believe me, perfection's just a word. As a general thing, it doesn't exist. It has to do with potential — and that's different for everybody. What's important is providing the proper atmosphere so that each person is eager to try for it." He took a deep breath. "Sorry," he said. "I didn't mean to give a lecture."

Jennifer grinned. "That's okay," she said. "No one's perfect."

Chapter 5

Nora set her hamster, Sinbad, back in his terrarium on top of her bookcase. Then she flopped down on top of her bedspread and plumped the pillows behind her head. Settling back against them, she reached for the pink calico cat cushion Jennifer had made for her birthday. She placed it on her outstretched legs with her phone on top. Although she had left the Manns' house only two hours earlier, she was impatient to talk to Jennifer.

"Hi, Nora," Jennifer answered on the second ring.

"One of these days, it's not going to be me," Nora said.

"Who else?" Jennifer said. "Steve already called."

Nora sat up. "Steve called? When?"

"Oh, a few minutes ago." Jennifer tried

to sound casual but she was bursting with excitement.

"What'd he want?"

Jennifer twisted her pink princess phone cord around her finger. "To talk," she said.

"What about?"

"This and that."

"Jennifer!" Nora exploded.

Jennifer laughed. "I couldn't resist," she teased. "You get so aggravated when I don't tell you everything right away."

"That's all right." Nora pretended to be offended. "I don't really want to know what he said anyway. I was only being polite." Giggling, she added, "If you believe that, I've got some tickets to the moon I'll sell you cheap."

"Thanks, but I'd rather stay on Earth and talk to Steve." Jennifer sighed. "He has the neatest voice."

"Jen! Tell me what he said!"

Jennifer settled into her red beanbag chair. "He's in charge of food for the judges."

"So what else is new?" Nora asked.

Like his father, who was in the restaurant business, Steve was interested in food selection and preparation.

"He wanted to know what *we're* doing so he can plan what *he's* doing."

"What *are* we doing?" Nora asked.

"I've been thinking about what Jeff said — that business about providing the right atmosphere."

Nora sank back against her pillows. "I've been thinking about it, too," she said, her tone flat. "The only way we can do that is move everybody to Hubbard Woods."

"Forget that," Jennifer said.

"So we lose." Nora sounded resigned.

"Nora!" Jennifer reprimanded. "Don't be so negative."

"I'm trying to be realistic, Jen," Nora said. "But no matter how I figure it, reality — in this case! — equals negative."

Jennifer got to her feet. "But you never give up without a fight, Nora."

That was true. It was one of Nora's strong points. Usually, however, Nora felt there was at least a chance of winning.

"But, this time, the match isn't . . . even," she said. "I mean Cedar Groves against Hubbard Woods! Not to mention the three other schools! It's impossible!"

Jennifer carried the phone to her desk. "The selection committee must have thought Cedar Groves had something, or we wouldn't have made the finals."

"It'd sure help if we knew what that was," Nora said.

Jennifer sat down and opened her desk drawer. Under her treasure box was a notepad. "We don't, so what we have to do is see what can be improved."

Nora sighed heavily. "Everything!"

"Jeff said we shouldn't expect perfection, remember?" Jennifer marked a piece of paper, THINGS TO BE IMPROVED. "What we should do is make a list of things we *can* do to make Cedar Groves seem as perfect as possible."

"Your ideas about the banners would — " Nora broke off. Out of the corner of her eye, she saw a blur of movement. "Jen, Sinbad got out! I forgot to close the lid. I've got to go! If my mother finds out he's loose — !"

"Meet me tomorrow early," Jennifer said. "We'll go through school and see what else needs doing."

"Okay," Nora said. "Oh, Jen? What're you wearing?"

"The T-shirt you gave me," Jennifer answered. The white shirt had been a Christmas present. It read: SO MUCH TO DO, SO LITTLE TIME. Jennifer often wore it to her meetings. "After all, this is a project."

"Probably the biggest one you've ever had!" Nora added before she hung up.

"Did you come up with any more ideas?" Nora asked Jennifer the next morning when they met on the corner near school.

But Jennifer wasn't listening; she was distracted by the striped oxford cloth shirt visible under Nora's open windbreaker and by the small string tie under the button-down collar. They were perfect compliments to Nora's camel-colored cords.

"Where'd you get the shirt?" Jennifer asked.

"Sally," Nora said. "Does it look okay?"

"It looks great. Very . . . businesslike."

"That's why I wore it," Nora explained. "We have a lot of business to attend to."

Jennifer laughed. "That's for sure."

"So what do we do first?" Nora asked.

"I thought we'd go inside now and — "

"Before the bell rings?" Nora interrupted. No self-respecting eighth-grader went inside school until the bell rang no matter what. It was an unwritten eighth grade rule.

"If we don't go through school now and make a list," Jennifer said, "we'll never have time."

They turned into the school walk. Except for Jason and his skateboard, none of their crowd had arrived yet.

"If we hurry, nobody'll even know," Jennifer said as she started up the front steps.

"Hey! Nora! Jen! What's your hurry?" Jason called after them.

The girls darted through the double doors without looking back.

"Now what?" Nora asked.

"Well, I think we should sort of pretend we're the judges," Jennifer responded.

Nora nodded. Her short dark curls bounced. "And look at the place as though we're seeing it for the first time." She patted her friend on the back. "Jen, you're a genius."

"Just logical," Jennifer demurred. She dug a small yellow spiral notebook out of her bookbag and shook a stubby pencil from its spine.

Nora took a few tentative steps down the corridor. The dark green tile floor was worn and cracked, but it was polished to a gleam. "I suppose the hall's all right. I mean it's already Wednesday; we couldn't retile the whole thing by Monday."

"We just have to keep people from looking down," Jennifer said. She focused on the walls, which were lined with class pictures going back to the first Cedar Groves Junior High graduating class.

Nora moved slowly from picture to picture. "Would you believe the way some of these people look!" she said.

"The glass is so dirty, it's hard to tell." Jennifer noted *Clean glass on pictures in hall* on the first page of the spiral.

"Look at this one, Jen."

Jennifer stepped back and cocked her head.

"Would you believe the hair!" Nora exclaimed.

"The early sixties," Jennifer commented as she searched her mind for trivia from the period. "Didn't they call that style a beehive?"

Nora giggled. "They all look like coneheads!"

"Even Mia looks better than these girls," Jennifer commented.

"*Andy* looks better than these girls!" Nora amended.

Studying the pictures intently, Jennifer moved along the hall. It was the first time either of the girls had paid any attention to the old photos. "These are really great!"

"There's Sally!" Nora exclaimed. The stern image of her sister stared into space above Nora's head.

"She looks awful," Jennifer said. "Why isn't she smiling?"

"She hardly ever smiled then," Nora said. "Don't you remember? She kept saying no one understood her."

The bell rang and the doors opened like flood gates.

"We didn't accomplish a thing," Jennifer complained as she got caught up in the tide of students. "What are we going to do?"

"Just keep your eyes open," Nora said, "and we'll compare notes later."

Mr. Mario stopped them at the door to room 332. "Have you decided on anything you'd like to do for Monday?" he asked.

Jennifer shifted from one foot to the other. "Well, not exactly," she said. "We started making a list this morning, but we got all involved in — "

"We do know we'd like to put up some banners," Nora interrupted. She didn't see any sense in letting Mr. Mario know they'd wasted so much time. "We need some people to make them."

Mr. Mario thought about that. Finally, he said, "All right. That'd be fine." Then, he turned and went to his desk where he clapped for attention.

Everyone scurried to their places. Jason sat head and shoulders above the rest of the class.

"Mr. Anthony," the teacher said, "have you grown suddenly or aren't you sitting?"

Jason shook his head and then nodded.

Mr. Mario sighed his I-don't-believe-what-I'm-seeing sigh. "Is that an answer?"

"It's two answers," Jason said.

"We need only one," Mr. Mario said.

"You asked two questions," Jason reminded him.

Resting his left elbow in his right palm, the teacher dropped his chin into his left palm and glared at Jason over the top of his glasses.

"No, I haven't grown suddenly," Jason continued, "and yes, I'm sitting."

"On what?" Mr. Mario demanded.

The class snickered.

Jason sheepishly pulled his skateboard out from under him and lowered himself into his chair. "I didn't have time to go to my locker," he said.

"Get rid of that board now," Mr. Mario directed.

"Yes, sir," Jason said and he skipped out of the room.

Jennifer wrote *skateboard* on her list. Then she tore out a sheet of paper and wrote Nora a note: *Nora, what are we going to do about Jason's board?!!*

As she was passing it across the aisle, Mr. Mario said, "Jennifer, Nora, are you ready?"

Jennifer withdrew the note guiltily. "For what, Mr. Mario?" she asked.

"To make your announcement," he said.

Jennifer looked at Nora, who shrugged.

"I was under the impression you wanted to enlist help in preparing for Monday."

Nora shot up. "Oh, you mean the banners." She turned to face the class. "Jennifer and I — we thought it'd be nice to put up some banners."

"What kind of banners?" Tommy wanted know.

From her place, Jennifer said, "Ones

48

that say 'You Are Entering Cedar Groves Junior High — ' "

Mitch guffawed. "They'll know that."

The class laughed. Mitch smiled smugly.

Jennifer stood up. "You didn't let me finish," she said.

"Yes, Mr. Pauley. Please, let her finish," Mr. Mario instructed.

Jennifer repeated, " 'You Are Entering Cedar Groves Junior High,' " adding, " 'Welcome!' " as she stared pointedly at Mitch.

"How about 'Welcome to Cedar Groves Junior High'?" Denise suggested.

"Or 'Cedar Groves Junior High Welcomes You.' " Tracy piped up.

Everyone murmured approval.

Tommy's mouth dropped open. "Who said that? Not our own Tracy Douglas?"

Tracy blushed and dropped her chin so that her long blonde hair fell over her face. "What's wrong with it?" she asked softly.

"Nothing!" Tommy said. "It's just such a surprise to discover one more of your talents."

Mr. Mario cleared his throat. He said, "I suggest we move on," but everyone knew it was more than a suggestion.

"We can figure out what the banners should say later," Nora said. "What we have to do now is figure out who's going to make them."

"Are there any other jobs?" Mitch wanted to know.

"We're not sure yet," Nora said.

Jennifer consulted her list. "The glass on all the class pictures in the main hall has to be cleaned," she said. Turning to Mr. Mario, she added, "Unless we can get the janitors to do it."

Mr. Mario shook his head. "They have enough to do."

Mitch raised his hand. "I'll make banners," he said.

Everyone's hand shot up. "Banners," they all said.

"Everyone can't make banners," Nora objected.

The bell rang. Instantly, people scattered, talking excitedly as they headed for the door.

"Meet back here after school!" Jennifer called above the noise.

"Jen, are you crazy?" Nora asked as she gathered her books. "Who wants to stay after?"

"We have to," Jennifer told her. "Time is running out!"

Chapter 6

Nora and Jennifer ducked into the girls' room on the way to first period.

"What are we going to do?" Jennifer asked as she tucked stray strands of hair into her ponytail. She had expected things to go smoothly. She'd make a list of things to be done and they'd get done. That's what she did with her projects. It had always worked. With them, of course, the list was for herself. The work load on this list was to be shared. Obviously, making lists for other people was tricky.

"We can't let people volunteer, that's for sure," Nora said. "They'll all want the same job. We'll just have to assign things."

"We'd better make sure we find the right people for the right jobs," Jennifer said. "Like for the posters — we can't let Mitch do those!" She made a notation in her book. "Who do you think'd be good?"

Nora wasn't listening. Her attention was on the ceiling. Once white, it was now gray, and, in one corner, the paint was flaking. "What're we going to do about this room?" she wondered. "The ceiling looks diseased."

"And this faucet leaks," Jennifer said as she gave the knob a turn.

"And the locks on a couple of stalls are broken," Nora added as she checked the doors.

As she made each notation, Jennifer felt herself gradually losing confidence. "It's impossible," she commented. "How are we ever going to do all of this?"

Nora, on the other hand, felt more positive than she had in days. Her face set with determination, she marched to the door. "Don't worry, Jen," she said. "We'll find a way."

All morning, the girls observed carefully — the shade in Mr. Rochester's room was torn; on Mr. Mario's world map, Italy had a gaping hole in the toe of the boot; clothing and papers hung out of overstuffed lockers; gum was stuck to the bottom of the gym locker room benches — and made notes.

"This place is worse than I thought," Jennifer said as she and Nora hurried to lunch.

"Some of it we might not have to worry about," Nora assured her. "Maybe the judges will all be men. That way we won't have to do anything about the girls' room."

"But they might all be women. And the boys' room is probably worse," Jennifer said. "There's nothing we can do about that!"

"We'll ask one of the boys to check it out," Nora suggested.

Jennifer made a notation. "Maybe we could ask Brad to do that."

A horrified expression swept over Nora's face. She couldn't ask Brad to do that. "Or Steve," she said.

"Steve's doing the food," Jennifer reminded her.

"Well, someone from our own homeroom then."

Jennifer stuffed her notebook into her back pocket and picked up a tray. "Who?" she asked. "We can't trust Jason — he'd play some kind of trick. And Tommy and Mitch. . . ." Her voice trailed off as Marc Johnson appeared beside her.

"Hi," he said.

Nora poked Jennifer and cocked her head toward him, a question in her eyes.

Jennifer shook her head. Marc Johnson had transferred from California early in the year. Although good-looking and affable, he was definitely not dependable.

Nora nodded. Jennifer was right.

"Forget I said 'hi,'" Marc said, observing the silent exchange between the two girls. "I didn't know you'd taken a vow of silence."

As he picked up his tray and slipped farther up in line, Nora and Jennifer laughed.

They sobered quickly when they sat down at their usual table.

"Oh, no!" Nora exclaimed. "Gum!" Strands of the sticky pink mass had attached to her as she sat down. She took a knife from her tray and began scraping at her jeans.

Jennifer crinkled her nose. "Why do people do that?"

"Don't look at me," Mia said. "That's bubble gum. I don't chew that. See." She stuck out her tongue, a wad of gum at the tip.

"Please. I'm trying to eat here," Susan said.

"Who uses this table during the early lunch periods?" Nora asked. She rubbed her thumb and forefinger together to dislodge the bits of gum stuck to her fingertips.

No one knew.

Jennifer sighed and dug out her notepad.

"What're you doing, Jen?" Amy asked.

"Making a list of the things that have to

be done before Monday," Jennifer told her.

"You sure are making a lot of work for yourselves," Lucy commented.

"Oh, we're not going to do it," Jennifer said. "Our job is showing the judges around."

Lucy looked puzzled. "Then why're you making the list?"

"So we can tell people what has to be done," Jennifer explained.

"What people?" Amy asked.

Jennifer shrugged. "People from our homeroom."

"Anybody really," Nora said. "Mr. Mario didn't say we had to stick to homeroom."

"That's right," Jennifer agreed. "All he said was we should check with him about what we planned to do."

"You mean you expect eighth-graders to scrape gum from under the cafeteria tables?" Denise asked. Her beautiful heart-shaped face was twisted in an expression of distaste.

"And off the benches in the locker room," Nora added.

The girls looked at one another in disbelief.

Mia fanned out her hands. Her long silver-polished nails were filed to sharp points. "What? And break my fingernails?"

"Actually, Mia," Susan said, "you'd be the perfect one for the job. You wouldn't even need a knife."

Mia dropped her nail polish, her mousse, her body streaker, and a wrapped Ho-Ho into her metal lunchbox/purse. "Ha," she said as she stood up. "I'd say 'ha-ha', but that remark only deserves half a laugh."

Denise got to her feet. "If you ask me, none of this is very funny," she said.

Lucy and Amy agreed as, grumbling, they cleared their places and readied to leave.

Tracy's wide blue eyes took in the scene. "Where's everybody going?" she asked. "The bell didn't even ring."

"Wait!" Jennifer said as the girls fell into formation to parade off. "There're lots of other jobs."

"Like what?" Lucy asked.

Jennifer consulted her list.

"We're having a meeting after school," Nora said. "Come to that and you'll find out. Originally, we planned the meeting only for our homeroom, but I think it'd be all right if you guys came, too, don't you, Jen?"

Jennifer closed her notebook. Nora was a genius. If she'd told the girls what was on the list, no one would be at the meeting. This way, they'd come out of curiosity. "Oh, I think it'd be okay." She tried not

56

to sound anxious. "All the best jobs'll be assigned at the meeting. And like we said, Mr. Mario didn't say we had to choose just from homeroom."

The girls looked at one another uncertainly. They were obviously weighing the situation. On the one hand, they didn't want to be involved. On the other, they were curious and wanted to be a part of things.

Sensing their ambivalence, Nora said, "Remember: school spirit."

"You want to win, don't you?" Jennifer added.

They all agreed they did. Still, attending the meeting might be going too far.

"We'll think about it," Denise said for them all.

Tracy looked stunned. "You have to come, Denise; you're in our homeroom."

Denise considered that. She supposed Tracy was right. Mr. Mario would probably be at the meeting; he might even take roll. She glanced at the others. "*They'll* think about it," she amended. Then, she turned and led the march out of the cafeteria.

"What do you think?" Jennifer asked Nora.

Nora smiled smugly. "They'll be there," she said.

* * *

Nora was right. The girls appeared at the door of room 332 soon after the last bell had rung. And they weren't the only ones: People from other homerooms who'd heard about the meeting through the eighth-grade grapevine showed up, too. Among them were Brad and Steve, who stood at the back of the room side by side.

While Mr. Mario called the meeting to order, Jennifer took several deep breaths to quiet the fluttering inside her. She didn't think she could trust herself to stand up in front of this large group with Steve's blue eyes watching her.

"You go first, Nora," she whispered.

Nora shook her head. "You've got the list."

"But Steve's back there."

"So is Brad!"

"And now Jennifer Mann and Nora Ryan have the floor," Mr. Mario said.

"Can I have the ceiling?" Tommy asked. Then he laughed.

No one else did.

The girls exchanged we're-in-this-together glances and moved to the front of of the room.

Jennifer pulled her ponytail over her shoulder and twisted a section around her finger. She opened her mouth to speak, but just then Steve smiled at her, and she forgot what she wanted to say.

Squaring her shoulders, Nora fixed her eyes on Joan Wesley, who was sharing a seat with Tracy. Still, she could see Brad out of her peripheral vision. She cleared her throat. "We all want to help Cedar Groves become Model Junior High of the Year," she began.

"Right on!" several voices piped up.

"And so," Nora continued, "Jennifer and I have made a list of things that have to be done by Monday." She turned to Jennifer, who looked at her blankly. "Jen? Where's the list?"

Jennifer's hazel eyes widened. Then they darted from side to side as she flipped through her mind trying to remember what she'd done with her notebook. Finally, she remembered. "It's on my desk." She retrieved it quickly and opened it to her list. "There're the posters," she said.

Most of the hands in the room shot up.

"We've decided to assign the jobs," Nora told the group. "Denise and Tracy are good in art."

Denise and Tracy smiled at one another.

"We'll need more than two people," Jennifer said. "We want posters in the front hall and in the cafeteria. Then there's the main bulletin board. We should do something special with that."

Mitch shot to his feet. "That bulletin board's fine the way it is," he objected. His picture was on it above the athletic schedule.

"The judges see your picture first thing, Pauley, and it's all over," Jason said.

"Right," Tommy put in. "Now if my picture were up there...."

"Oh, yeah?" Mitch challenged.

Mr. Mario cleared his throat.

Frowning, Mitch dropped into his seat and crossed his arms over his chest.

"Denise and Tracy can pick people to help them," Nora said.

Tracy looked around the room. She smiled at Brad.

Nora panicked. She couldn't let Tracy loose with this responsibility. The girl'd choose boys only. More to the point, she'd choose Brad! "Denise, you be in charge," she added quickly.

"And remember to pick people with some ... artistic ability," Jennifer instructed.

Still smiling at Brad, Tracy said, "We'll need help hanging the banners."

Nora glanced around the room quickly. Her eyes fell on Jason's red hair. "Jason's in charge of that," she said as though that decision had been made long ago.

"Yeah!" Jason said relishing the idea of working with Denise and Tracy.

"I'll help with that job," Tommy offered. His tone suggested he was doing them all a favor.

"Jason's in charge," Nora said. "You'll have to talk to him."

Jason tossed a smug glance at Tommy, who curled his lip in response.

"What else, Jen?" Nora asked.

As Jennifer read through her list, a heavy silence fell over the group. She finished reading and looked around the room for a reaction. Stunned eyes stared back at her.

Finally, Jason let out a long, audible breath. "This place should be condemned."

Chapter 7

"I don't think this is going to work," Jennifer said after the meeting.

Nora disagreed. "A piece of cake," she said. "Everyone grumbles a lot, but — "

"That's for sure," Jennifer broke in.

The meeting had been long and chaotic. Every suggestion was argued; every decision railed against. Under a shower of complaints, Jennifer and Nora had left room 332 hurriedly and ducked into the rock room where no one would look for them. Originally a storage room, the small space housed shelves on which were displayed various kinds of rocks. It shared a wall with the girls' lounge from which, even now, a continuing barrage of complaints pelted them through the wall.

"Once they get it out of their systems," Nora said, "they'll come through."

"I sure hope you're right," Jennifer responded doubtfully.

"And Mr. Mario's made it easier," Nora reminded her friend.

That was true. For one thing, he had forbidden them to so much as think about fixing plumbing. "That's a job for experts," he said, "and the selection committee will use faculty facilities." He suggested they forget about the gum, too, explaining that it would take too much time. "Perhaps we could ask for volunteers to do it over the summer," he said, adding, "The next *several* summers," after the girls had made clear the magnitude of the job. He'd taken a red pencil to Jennifer's list finally. What remained were those jobs he defined as, "Sprucing up the place a bit."

"At least we got the banners assigned," Jennifer said as she glanced over her list. "And Mr. Mario said he'd take care of his map." She laughed, remembering his exact words: "I'll . . . see a shoemaker. Perhaps he can recommend a way to mend the toe of the boot." Then, she continued, "But we never even got to the people. Mia and Andy's clothes and Jason's skateboard — we never got to those things."

"Shhh!" Nora said, her head cocked toward the girls' lounge. "Listen to that!"

"Nora and Jen are the bossiest people I

ever met!" Joan Wesley's voice came through loud and clear.

Jennifer's mouth dropped open. She couldn't believe what she was hearing. *Joan Wesley* was the bossiest person in the whole school! When anyone thought Joan, they thought bossy. The two words went together like Jason and skateboard. "She should talk!"

Nora waved her to silence.

"This job has certainly gone to their heads." Denise!

"Denise?" Jennifer said incredulously. Denise rarely criticized anyone — certainly not Jen and Nora, who considered her their second best friend.

"And we put her in charge of the banners!" Nora said.

Jennifer put a finger to her lips. "Shh. Listen."

"It doesn't take much for something to go to *their* heads," Susan was saying. "There's so much space up there."

Jennifer looked stricken.

Nora dismissed that comment with, "Oh, well, Susan." She was about to add, "No one'll pay any attention to *her*," when the sound of laughter drowned out the thought.

Unwilling to face their classmates after what they'd overheard, Jennifer and Nora waited until there was no sound from the next room before they sneaked out into the hall. It was as empty as it had been this morning when they arrived. And like this morning, dusty beams of light seemed to bar their way. They trudged through them silently, each wishing Mr. Mario had chosen someone else to host the selection committee.

As they turned the corner to their lockers, Jason catapulted off his skateboard right into them.

Nora's books flew out of her arms, one of them hitting Jason on the head. "Watch it, jerk!" she snapped.

Jason rubbed his forehead. "The hostess with the mostest," he said sarcastically.

Jennifer squatted to help Nora gather her books. "Very funny," she said.

Jason caught up with his runaway board, hopped on, and disappeared around the corner. The clack of his wheels was the only sound as the girls continued on their way.

Nora had exchanged her afternoon class books for the ones she needed for homework before she said, "You know, Jen, I think we're concentrating on the wrong things."

Stuffing her backpack, Jennifer paused, and gave Nora a questioning look.

"The banners and all that — it's all fine; I think we should do that, but if nothing else changes, what good will it do?"

Jennifer nodded. Nora was expressing her own fear.

"So the school looks great . . . better anyway . . . and Jason comes screaming around a corner on his skateboard and Mia and Andy show up looking like refugees from some punk band and — "

" — Joan doesn't let anybody else answer in class," Jennifer broke in, "and Tommy goes around combing his hair in public."

Nora nodded. "It's the *people* who need changing. And we never even got to them at the meeting."

"That's what I said before," Jennifer reminded her.

"Well, it's our responsibility to do something about it." Nora slammed her locker door for emphasis.

By the time they had reached the side door, both girls were talking at once. Their enthusiasm for the job had not died, as they had thought, it had only taken a fall. But it was up now, on its feet, ready for the good fight.

At the corner where each turned a different direction toward home, Nora said, "If you make a list of all the people who need changing — "

"That's, like, everybody!" Jennifer put in.

"No way we can change the whole eighth grade," Nora said. "Just the worst cases."

Jennifer fished out her notebook and scratched WORST CASES at the top of a fresh page. Then, she frowned. This was different from her other projects; they had to do with changing things, not people. "What're we going to do with the list?"

"I'll call you tonight and we'll go over it to be sure you didn't leave anybody out and then. . . ." Nora's voice trailed off. She wasn't sure what they'd do after that. "We'll figure it out," she said, trusting that once they knew exactly *what* they were dealing with, they'd know *how* to deal with it.

Jennifer responded with a determined nod. Nora was right: They would figure it out. Her method had always worked before; it would work now. She stashed the notebook in her jacket pocket. "Okay," she said. "Talk to you later."

At home, Jennifer grabbed a couple of cookies from the Garfield cookie jar on the counter and headed for her room, taking the stairs two at a time.

Jeff appeared in the hall below her. "How was your day?" he asked.

The question pulled her up short. Instantly, the conversation she and Nora had overheard replayed in her head. Did the other girls talk about her and Nora like that all the time? she wondered. She couldn't answer Jeff's question. If she did, she might cry. She sighed.

Jeff chuckled. "That bad, huh?" he said, adding "If you want to talk about it, you know where to find me," as he drifted into the kitchen.

Jennifer continued up the stairs slowly. A fireball raged in the pit of her stomach. It had never before occurred to her that people might talk about her behind her back. Judging by Nora's stunned reaction, it had never occurred to Nora either. But Nora had snapped back quickly. By now, she'd probably forgotten all about the incident.

As Jennifer entered her room, her image slid into the long mirror over her dresser. She looked at it for a long time. It stared back at her, twisting strands of dark hair around an index finger. There was a challenge in her image's eyes. "You're being ridiculous," Jennifer told herself. "You're just. . . . overreacting." Her image continued to glare at her.

She turned her back on the reflection and crossed the room to the desk under her windows. Her crystal whale caught a few stray beams of light and broke them into small rainbowed puddles.

Sighing, she sat down and pulled the notebook out of her jacket pocket. The heading WORST CASES seemed to shout at her. She turned the notebook over.

Nora didn't think about the overheard conversation again until she got home. Then it popped out of the shadows of her mind like a monster in an amusement park haunted house. And it startled her just as much. How could her friends talk about her that way? She and Jennifer were trying to do a good job — that was all. It wasn't fair to be made the object of ridicule for that.

She opened the refrigerator door, looked in without seeing, then let the door swing shut. She rummaged around in the cabinets, coming up with a candy bar, which she unwrapped without thinking, and began to munch.

At the doorway between the kitchen and the family room, Sally let out a surprised gasp. "Am I seeing what I think I'm seeing?" she asked. "No. Can't be," she went on without waiting for an answer. "Nora Ryan does not eat candy bars."

Horrified, Nora glanced down at her hand. "Candy!" she exclaimed and dropped the bar on the counter as if it were too hot to handle.

Sally laughed. "It's okay," she said. "I promise I won't talk about it behind your back."

Nora recoiled as if Sally had just struck her. "How could you say that?" she snapped and tore out of the room.

"Hey, Nor," Sally called after her. "I was only teas — "

Nora slammed her bedroom door.

Sinbad poked his head up through the nest of cloth scraps he'd piled in a corner of his terrarium. He darted to his exercise wheel and began running inside it. The wheel went faster and faster, but no matter how fast he ran, Sinbad stayed in exactly the same place.

"Let's hear your list," Nora said when she called Jennifer after supper.

Jennifer glanced at her notebook. It lay facedown on top of her desk where she had put it after school. "I didn't get to it yet." She didn't explain that she'd felt reluctant to put people's names on a list headed WORST CASES. Nora wouldn't understand. She wasn't sure she herself understood.

Fortunately, Nora didn't press. Instead, she said, "I've been thinking about it, and I've decided we have to call another meeting."

A jolt of panic shot through Jennifer. "I

don't think it'd be a good idea to . . . read the list or anything like that," she said.

"Hardly," Nora said. "They'd *really* talk about us if we did that."

Nora had not forgotten the incident either! Jennifer giggled with relief. "Can't you just hear them?"

"Please, Jen," Nora said. "I heard them once. That was enough!"

"I felt real bad about it," Jennifer confessed. "I mean it really . . . hurt."

"*Moi, aussi,*" Nora said. Using the French to indicate she, too, had felt awful seemed to put distance between her and her bad feelings, lessening their impact. She hated to dwell on bad feelings. They could sap a person's energy, and she and Jen needed all the energy they could muster to carry out their job.

Jennifer giggled again as the tension bubbled out of her. "So what are we going to do?" she asked.

"I thought maybe we could . . . sort of make general rules." Nora began to pace between her bookshelves and her bed. "Like a dress code — things like that."

Jennifer's eyes widened. "A dress code," she repeated to be sure she understood Nora's point. "That way we wouldn't have to mention Mia and Andy directly."

"Right," Nora said. "It'd be for everybody. I mean, Denise overdresses, if you ask me."

"You think so?" Jennifer asked. "I think she looks great. Lucy, too."

"It's different with Lucy," Nora argued. "She always looks terrific, but — "

"That's because she knows how to put everything together," Jennifer put in, wishing she could do the same.

"But Denise is . . . showy," Nora said. "She always has to have the best."

"She can afford it!"

"Yeah, Jen, but do you think it's good to have one person stand out like that?"

Jennifer shrugged. "She's so pretty she'd stand out no matter what she wore."

Nora felt a twinge of guilt. Was she criticizing Denise out of spite? "Well, anyway," she said to redirect the focus, "we should probably talk about a dress code."

"I think you're right, Nora. What else?"

"I'm not sure. I mean there's Jason and that skateboard, but I don't know how to make up a general rule about that."

Jennifer laughed. "There is one already!" Skateboards were forbidden by school rule; yet Jason got away with riding his in the halls.

"Maybe we could just talk to him privately or something," Nora suggested.

"That might work," Jennifer said. "He

did give it up for a while when his ankle was broken."

"Only because Mr. Donovan took it away from him," Nora reminded her.

In her mind's eye, Jennifer saw Jason, his foot in a cast, careening awkwardly down the front hall right into Mr. Donovan. The scene made her smile.

"It's probably hopeless," Nora said.

"If we make him see how important it is. . . ."

"You talk to him, Jen."

"Why me?"

"You have more . . . patience with him. He listens to you."

"Jason doesn't listen to anybody, but I'll try." Jennifer crossed the room to her desk. "I better get this stuff down." She turned her notebook over. She wrote: *1. Dress Code (Mia and Andy—Denise?) 2. Skateboard (Jason)*. "Okay. Now what else?"

Before long, Jennifer had filled several sheets in her small notebook under the heading WORST CASES.

Chapter 8

When Nora and Jennifer turned up the walk to school, Tommy and Mitch fell into step behind them.

"What terrific jobs do you think they'll have for us today?" Tommy asked loudly.

"Some little thing like building a new school," Mitch answered.

Jennifer shot them a sour look.

They laughed and ran past the girls to the front steps.

"They are so annoying," Jennifer commented.

Nora's attention was elsewhere. "Would you just look at her!" she said.

Jennifer glanced around. Their friends were gathered on the steps in small groups. The boys — except for Jason, who was doing hand plants on the soggy lawn — hovered nearby. Nothing seemed out of the ordinary. "Who?" she asked.

"Denise Hendrix!" Nora hissed.

Denise stood on a lower step talking to Tracy. She wore straight-leg ice-washed jeans, a matching oversized jacket and a cornflower blue turtleneck. A ribbon, in a darker shade of blue, caught her long blonde hair loosely at the back of her head. She smiled and waved as Nora and Jen approached.

"Can you believe her?" Nora snapped.

By the time she and Jennifer had finished their phone conversation last night, Nora thought she'd finally gotten over her hurt feelings. After all, everyone said mean things once in a while. If she was honest, she'd have to admit she had made an occasional unkind remark herself. Denise certainly hadn't meant to be cruel. A person often found it hard to accept a close friend in a role of authority. Best thing was to forget what she and Jen had heard. But seeing Denise dredged up yesterday's hurt with a difference: Now, it felt like anger.

Misunderstanding Nora's meaning, Jennifer said, "It is hard to believe anybody could be that beautiful."

"Jen!" Nora said, impatience edging her voice. "How can you be so nice?"

Jennifer was puzzled. "Nice?" she said. "More like, truthful."

"But she's . . . smiling! Doesn't that

75

make you sick?" Nora felt that would clarify her meaning. Just hours ago, Denise had talked behind their backs and now she was smiling at them as though nothing had happened.

Still missing the point, Jennifer nodded. "Sort of. I mean her smile is so perfect. Her teeth are so perfect. Everything's perfect!"

Nora shook her head. "Jen, think! Yesterday, Denise — "

Denise ran up to them. "Watching you two come up that walk was like watching a movie in slow motion," she said and laughed.

Nora took a deep breath.

"Here's a list of the people on our committee," Denise said.

Nora looked down at the sheet of notebook paper Denise held out toward her and then up at Denise. There was nothing in the older girl's face to indicate discomfort. How could she be so cool after what she'd said yesterday?

After a pause, Denise asked, "You want it or what?"

Jennifer glanced at Nora. Her face was tight, her eyes angry. She reached out for Denise's list. "I'll take it."

Denise didn't hear her. Her attention was fixed on Nora. "What's wrong, Nora?" she asked, genuine concern in her voice.

Jennifer took the list from Denise's hand. "I'm the list person," she said lightly, hoping to lessen the tension.

"You look mad." Denise said to Nora.

Nora glanced away. "Mad? Me?" she said. "Why should I be mad?"

Denise shrugged. "I don't know why," she said. "I don't even know if you are. You look it is all I said. I thought maybe the boys — "

"The *boys* have nothing to do with this," Nora snapped.

"Well, pardon me," Denise said, and then she marched to the top of the stairs where she joined Lucy and Amy.

When the three of them glanced down at her, Nora turned her back. "She's doing it again!" she growled.

"Doing what again?"

"Talking about us — *that's* what!"

Jennifer looked from the girls to Nora and back again. The three girls were engaged in conversation with Mitch and Tommy. They didn't seem the least bit interested in her or Nora.

"They're talking to the boys," Jen assured her friend.

"About us!" Nora shot back.

Jennifer took a deep breath. There was no sense arguing. When Nora got an idea into her head, nothing could get it out. She slipped her notebook out of her pocket. "I finished the list," she said, purposely changing the subject.

Nora took it from her. As she read through the list, her face relaxed. By the time she reached the end, she was smiling. "You got 'em all!" she said, sounding smugly satisfied.

Since Jennifer couldn't stay after school that day, and Nora couldn't stay after the next, they decided to hold their second meeting at lunchtime. They announced their plan during homeroom period.

"Why do we need another meeting?" Tommy wanted to know.

Nora and Jennifer exchanged uncertain glances. Each hoped the other would come up with a satisfying answer.

"Because if it's about more jobs, I've already got one. I'm helping Jason hang banners," Tommy said.

"Right," Jason added. "The people who have jobs shouldn't have to be there."

"It's not about more jobs," Jennifer put in quickly. "It's about — " She broke off. If she told them the purpose of the meeting, no one would attend.

Recognizing her distress, Nora sprang to the rescue. "It's about ways to win," she said. "If we get together and talk about that, we'll probably come up with all sorts of ideas." She took a deep breath and held it. Would the class accept that?

For several seconds, uncertainty hung in the air. People looked at one another, attempting to gauge the collective reaction.

Finally, Denise spoke up. "I think that's a good idea," she said. "That way we can all make suggestions."

Then everyone started talking at once.

Nora cocked her head toward Jennifer and smiled triumphantly.

The bell rang.

"Pass the word," Nora told her classmates as they scurried out of the room.

At her desk, Jennifer asked, "Nora? Where's the notebook?"

Nora grabbed her books and headed for the door. "What notebook?"

"*My* notebook. The one with the lists."

"Where'd you put it?"

"You had it last. Outside, remember? You were looking at it when the bell rang."

"I gave it back."

"No, you didn't."

Nora glanced down the hall. "Come on, Jen. We'll be late."

Jennifer ran to the window. "Maybe you dropped it or something." She craned her neck toward the front entrance, but she was too far up to see clearly.

"It's probably in your jacket pocket," Nora said.

Jennifer thought about that. She did have a tendency to be forgetful sometimes, especially when she had a lot on her mind. She joined Nora at the door. "Maybe I should check."

Nora pulled her by the arm. "Not now. There isn't time."

Jennifer trotted along beside her friend. "You really think that's where it is?"

Nora said, "Trust me, Jen," as they slipped into English class at the moment the bell sounded.

Word of the meeting spread rapidly. Everyone was eager to make suggestions for increasing Cedar Groves's chances of winning. They stopped Nora and Jen between classes to say, "Count on me," or "I'll be there," or "Wait'll you hear *my* ideas!"

By fourth period gym, Nora had forgotten all about being angry with Denise and the other girls, and Jennifer had forgotten all about the missing notebook.

"You know, Jen," Nora said as she pulled on her shapeless blue gym shorts, "maybe I should be a politician instead of a doctor."

Thinking she was serious, Jennifer said, "You're not serious!"

Nora laughed. "Not really." She'd

wanted to be a doctor for as long as she could remember. Still, judging by this morning's experience, the prospect of "leading the people" was tempting. "I might be good at it, though," she said, heady with self-confidence. "I mean look what happened this morning. Nobody wanted another meeting and now everybody does. All it took was the right word." She leaned over to tie her Reeboks. "I guess being a good politician is a lot like being a good salesman."

Jennifer didn't share her certainty. It was obvious from the class reaction that everyone expected the meeting to be an open forum for the purpose of gathering ideas. No one realized that the ideas had already been gathered. "And what happens when everybody shows up to buy one thing and we give them another?" she asked.

Nora waved away that objection. "Trust me, Jen. Everybody wants to win. They'll be very cooperative."

After gym class, Nora went to ask Mr. Mario where they could meet. Room 332 was definitely too small for the expected crowd. He checked and found the resource room available.

"I won't be able to be there," he told her. "I have a test to run off for this afternoon's classes."

"That's okay," Nora assured him. "We can handle it."

She hurried to the cafeteria to spread the word. Jennifer met her at the door, a worried look on her face.

"The notebook's not in my jacket," Jennifer said urgently. "It's not anywhere in my locker!"

"Tell everybody the meeting's in the resource room," Nora told a passing group. To Jennifer she said, "Come on, if we don't eat right now, we won't have time." She started inside.

Jennifer caught her by the arm. "Nora! Did you hear what I said? The notebook's not in my — "

"I heard you, Jen. We don't need the notebook. We know the worst cases by heart."

Chapter 9

Jennifer hesitated just inside the cafeteria door when she saw Steve talking to Mia. He smiled and waved her over.

"Jen," Nora said, "you can't talk to Steve *now*! There isn't time!"

Jennifer said, "There's always time to talk to Steve."

Nora sighed. "Well, all right," she said, as though Jen had asked her permission. "I'll get you some lunch."

Jen drifted up beside Mia, who said, "Hi, Jen. I was just telling Steve he ought to plan something unusual for the judges."

"Like what?" Jennifer asked.

Steve laughed. "Are you ready for this? Bees!"

"And grasshoppers," Mia added.

Jennifer's eyes widened. "Sure," she said, her tone ironic.

"I'm serious," Mia snapped. "Why

doesn't anyone ever take me seriously?"
She marched off.

Steve smiled a cockeyed, amused grin.
"Yeah, Jen," he said, "why don't you ever
take Mia seriously? She looks serious,
doesn't she?"

The two of them watched Mia thread her
way to the girls' table. Her hair was mostly
blue today, pulled up into a single spike to
which a floppy green cabbage rose was attached.

Jennifer rolled her eyes. "Right."

At the table, Nora was gesturing to her.

Reluctantly, Jennifer edged away. "I
guess I'd better go."

Steve nodded. "You've got that meeting."

"You coming?" Jennifer asked.

"Can't," he answered. "I have to check
Monday's menu with Miss Morton."

Jennifer was relieved. It'd be easier to
get through this meeting without Steve
watching her every move. "Good thing
Mia's not the cooking teacher," she joked.

The sound of his laugh was still in her
head when she joined her friends at their
table.

"I heard grasshoppers are really good
covered with chocolate," Mia was saying.

"Gross me out," Lucy said.

"Lots of people eat grasshoppers," Nora
said.

The others looked at her skeptically.

"Really," Nora assured them. "They eat worms, too."

"Worms!" Amy shivered.

"Please! This is lunch — not biology!" Susan growled.

From the next table, Mitch piped up, "Who eats worms?"

Nora ignored him. "Maggots are actually considered a delicacy in some cultures." She turned to Jennifer, who sat with her fork poised above her tuna casserole. "Hurry up and eat, Jen. We can't be late for our own meeting."

Jennifer pushed her plate away. "I'm not hungry," she said.

Marc Johnson popped out of the rock room. When he saw Nora and Jennifer approaching on their way to the resource center, he popped back inside.

Jennifer paused and glanced back over her shoulder. The rock room door opened and Marc's head appeared. He motioned Tommy and Mitch, who were headed his way. Then, all three boys disappeared inside the room.

"Weird," Jennifer commented as she skipped to catch up to Nora.

The resource room chairs were turned upside down on the tables as though the room had been prepared for cleaning.

"Now what do we do?" Jennifer asked anxiously.

"Don't panic," Nora said, panic in her voice. There wasn't time to turn all the chairs right side up and people wouldn't stay if they had to stand up. "We'll just . . ." While she was trying to think of a solution, classmates began arriving. With a minimum of fuss, each righted a chair and sat down. ". . . let them do it," she concluded.

When everyone seemed to be there, Nora called the meeting to order.

"Ryder and Pauley aren't here," Jason objected.

"Marc Johnson's missing, too," one of the girls said.

"We can't wait forever," Nora said. She looked at Denise. "Let's start with a report on what's already been done."

Denise stood up. "Well, Tracy and I picked the committee. Jen has the list."

Jennifer's face underwent a series of changes as she tried to remember what she'd done with it. She remembered! Her mouth and shoulders settled into a droop. Denise's list was in the missing notebook.

"You lost it," Denise said. Her tone said, "I knew you would." She sighed and dug out her copy.

"That's okay," Nora said. "We don't need to take time reading the list or anything. As long as you're working on the banners."

"We aren't," Tracy piped up.

Denise shot her an impatient glance. "We're meeting tomorrow to do the planning," she said, "and we're going to work on them Saturday. No one had time to do it before then."

"And when are we supposed to put 'em up?" Jason asked.

"I don't know," Denise answered. "That's your job."

"You'll have to do it Sunday," Nora told Jason.

"Sunday!" he exploded. "They won't let us in this place on *Sunday*!"

"This is special," Nora told him. "We'll get permission." She turned to Jennifer, who stood behind her, twisting her hair. "Make a note of that, Jen," she said.

Jennifer said, "Right," and then, remembering she didn't have her book of lists, she asked, "Does someone have a piece of paper?"

Joan Wesley opened her notebook and handed Jennifer two sheets. "I suppose you need a pencil, too." She used her most patronizing tone.

Jennifer felt herself redden. She murmured, "Thanks," and busied herself with her new list.

"Okay," Nora said, "so this meeting is

to talk about ideas to help us win, so" — several hands went up — "Jen and I'll give ours first."

As the hands went down, voices rose. No one thought the girls were being fair.

Nora stemmed the flood of objections with, "The whole thing was our idea." When the grumbling had trickled down to a few inaudible mumbles, she continued, "Jen'll go first."

"I will?" Jennifer's voice cracked. She cleared her throat. "That's okay. You're doing fine, Nora."

"Jen," Nora said between her teeth.

"Somebody start before the bell rings!" Joan Wesley called out.

Jennifer tossed her head, so that her ponytail fell back over her shoulder, and stepped forward. "Well, Nora and I — we thought it might be a good idea to set up some general rules." She paused. Without her notebook, she couldn't remember the exact wording of the rules.

Everyone stared at her expectantly.

She shot Nora a pleading glance.

Nora took a deep breath. "Like, for instance, clothes," she said.

That put Jennifer on firmer ground. "Right," she said. "We thought it'd be a good idea to have a kind of dress code."

An audible gasp swept through the room.

Nora held up her hand for silence. "That way no one will . . . stand out."

Jason was on his feet. "I suppose you'd be happy if we all wore uniforms." The disgust was heavy in his voice.

His comment made everyone laugh. Jason looked confused at first, but then he realized: He was wearing his camouflage jumpsuit — definitely a uniform! He sank back into his chair.

"What's so funny?" Mia broke in. "Most of the people in this class are wearing uniforms." Glancing around the room, her gaze fell on Denise and Lucy. "Those two! They look like something out of a preppy handbook." She nodded her head for emphasis; the green cabbage rose bobbed.

The laughter swelled.

Nora called for order. No one heard her.

In the confusion, Marc slipped in. Tommy and Mitch, their faces solemn, came in at his heels. Marc sat down beside Jason at the front of the room. The others found places at the back.

Marc nudged Jason. "Take a look at this," he said and passed Jason a small yellow spiral notebook.

Jason looked at the notebook without really seeing it. The only thing that registered was that it was in Jen's handwriting. He could tell by the small open circles over the i's. He handed it back.

"Pass it on," Marc whispered.

Jason shrugged and handed it to the person next to him.

Nora raised her voice. "Let's all think about it," she suggested. She knew it was pointless to continue discussion of a dress code now; they'd spend the entire period on that one rule and come to no conclusion. "We can talk more about it tomorrow. Remember the point is no one should stand out. That goes for everybody!"

"And that doesn't mean just clothes," Jennifer added. "There are other things, too, like answering in class. Poeple should give other people a chance to do that on Monday, and not just, you know, be the first one all the time." Her glance fell on Joan Wesley.

Thinking that rule was aimed at someone else, Joan glanced behind her. Tracy smiled at her. She faced front. Now, both Jen and Nora were looking directly at her. "Do you mean me?"

Jennifer shifted her weight from one foot to the other. "It's a kind of . . . general rule, but — "

"She means you," Tommy piped up.

Joan adjusted her glasses and drew her mouth into a thin, tight line. "I don't do that," she protested. She looked around for someone to support her. When no one did, she said, "Can I help it if I'm the only one who knows the answers?"

"You just think you know all the answers," Susan said.

"Another thing," Nora hastened to add. "We should be . . . nice to one another."

Jennifer nodded. "That's really important. We shouldn't be . . . sarcastic or anything."

Mitch hooted. "Guess who that means!"

Susan turned her head slowly to glare at him. "I *am* nice!" she barked. "Just because I'm *honest* — "

"We shouldn't take any of this personally," Nora broke in. "Remember the whole point is winning!"

Mia poked Andy, who sat beside her. She pointed to the first item on the page headed WORST CASES in the yellow notebook.

Their whispering caught Jennifer's attention. Suddenly, she felt very warm. Her mouth went dry and there was a strange buzzing in her ears. She steadied herself against the front table. Finally, her mind grasped what her senses already knew: Mia had her missing notebook!

"And we should be willing to do whatever we can to help Cedar Groves win," Nora was saying.

Mia shot to her feet. "No one's going to tell *me* how to dress!" she exploded. "Or

Andy either," she added as she urged him to his feet.

Confused by the outburst, Nora said, "We're not talking about the dress code anymore, Mia."

Jennifer poked Nora with her elbow. Nora frowned at her. Jennifer cocked her head toward the notebook.

Mia took Andy by the hand and pulled him toward the door, her nose in the air.

"You can't leave, Mia," Nora protested. "The meeting's not over!"

Jennifer cupped her hand over her mouth. "The notebook!" she hissed in Nora's direction.

Just then, Tracy popped up, the yellow spiral in her outstretched hand. "Jen?" she asked full of innocence. "Is this yours? It looks like your handwriting."

Jennifer stepped forward to accept the notebook. Grasping the situation finally, Nora blocked her way. "Maybe Mia's right," she said. "The bell's going to ring any minute." She took the notebook, glanced at it casually as though she hadn't the slightest idea what it was, and dropped it on the desk beside her. Then she smiled uneasily. "Maybe we can meet . . . tomorrow sometime."

No one moved.

"Meeting adjourned," she said lightly.

Still, no one stirred.

Nora eased toward the door. "Well, we're leaving. Right, Jen?"

Jennifer tried to move, but her feet seemed rooted to the floor.

Tommy Ryder whipped out his comb and pointedly drew it through his sandy hair. Finding his name in Jennifer's notebook had shocked him at first. Some of the others belonged there, he felt, but putting him on the list was certainly a mistake, and he wanted to make the girls squirm. "What about Jason?" he said.

"What about me?" Jason responded.

"You're in the book — one of the 'Worst Cases,'" Tommy explained.

Jason leaned over the table and snatched the book off the desk.

Finding the strength to uproot herself, Jennifer sprang toward him. "You give me that, Jason Anthony!"

People rushed forward to form a barrier between the two.

Jason saw the notation about skateboards immediately. Although he would not willingly surrender his skateboard to anyone, he had no intention of riding it through the halls on Monday. The fact that Nora and Jennifer thought he would hurt and angered him. He tried to think of something to say that would put them in their places, but he couldn't. Instead, he scanned the rest of the list. "'Dress Code:

Mia and Andy,'" he read. "Hey, Denise! You're included on that one, too!"

"*Me*?! Under *dress* code?!" Denise's tone contained equal parts of surprise and indignation.

"Relax, Denise," Jason said. "There's a question mark after your name. So they weren't so sure about you." He flipped to the next page. "Hey, Trace, you made the list, too!"

Tracy beamed as though she thought it was an honor. "I did?"

"Something about trying to act . . . smarter."

The corners of Tracy's mouth drooped. "Oh."

Nora cast an imploring glance at Jennifer — did *she* have any ideas? — but her friend seemed to have shrunk — to *be* shrinking right before her eyes.

"Jen!" she exclaimed. When Jen didn't respond, Nora knew she was on her own. Her expression knotted with determination. Her hands flew to her hips. "Listen, everybody!" she bellowed. "This is ridiculous. Everybody's on that list, practically. No one's *per*fect!"

"*Some* people sure *think* they are."

Neither Jennifer nor Nora was certain who said that, but they knew *every*one was thinking it.

Chapter 10

The bell rang.

The resource room emptied in a whirl-wind. In its wake, Jennifer and Nora stood alone, staring at the small yellow, spiral notebook. Neither of them moved to retrieve it from the floor where Jason had dropped it.

Nora was the first to break the silence. "If you hadn't lost that stupid note-book. . . ." Her voice trailed off, leaving the conclusive words unsaid.

But Jennifer understood the meaning: It was her fault the meeting had been such a disaster. She looked at her friend, her hazel eyes clouded with hurt.

Nora glanced away, but not before Jen-nifer saw the defiance on her face.

A wave of anger broke over Jennifer. "*Me*? You're the one who had it last, Nora Ryan!"

"I gave it back!"

"Did not!"

"Did, too!" Nora planted her feet far apart. "And besides, Jennifer, you're the one who wrote everything *down*."

"Because you told me to, Nora," Jennifer countered.

"That's ridiculous! You always write everything down!"

A few seventh-graders drifted into the room. They stood at the door, gawking at the girls.

Nora edged toward the door. "Really, Jen, that's a very bad habit — writing everything down like that."

The room was filling up.

"Maybe we should make a rule about *that*!" Nora put her nose in the air and stomped out of the room.

Jennifer scooped up the notebook. It felt like it was burning in her hand. She wanted to throw it away, forget it ever existed, but habit was strong, and she instinctively stuffed it into her denim bag as she pushed against the current of arriving seventh-graders.

She tore down the hall, calling, "Nora! Wait!"

Nora picked up her pace, her nose tipped so high, she was looking at the ceiling.

Jennifer caught up with her outside room 108. "You're not being fair," she said urgently. "I mean the whole thing about changing people — that was your idea!"

Nora opened her mouth to protest, then shut it. She couldn't honestly remember whose idea it had been. She and Jennifer had been so close for so long — since kindergarten! — that it was as if they shared one mind, exchanging ideas freely with no need to claim ownership. But Jennifer was trying to fix blame, and Nora refused to accept it. "So why'd you listen?" she challenged.

The bell rang, saving Jennifer from answering Nora's question, but nothing could save her from thinking about it.

Mr. Robards drew their attention to the board where he had written POLITICAL ETHICS. "Can anyone define this term?" he asked.

Joan Wesley's hand shot up. When Mr. Robards recognized her, she stood up and pushed at the bridge of her glasses with a forefinger. "Political ethics — " she sounded as though she were about to spell the words " — a set of moral principles having to do with a government." She sat down.

Mr. Robards nodded. "Questions?"

There were none.

He turned to the board and wrote, THE END NEVER JUSTIFIES THE MEANS. Then he stepped aside. "Anyone want to give this one a try?"

"It means that no matter how good the purpose, a person can't do things that are dishonest or hurtful to achieve it," Denise offered unexpectedly.

Mr. Robards looked pleased. "Does everyone understand that?" he asked.

Jennifer shifted in her chair. For some reason, this whole conversation was making her uncomfortable. She cast a troubled glance at Nora.

Feeling Jen's eyes on her, Nora put her hands up to either side of her face like blinders. She didn't want her friend to see the uneasiness that had been mounting inside her since the beginning of class.

"All right," Mr. Robards said as he brushed at the chalk on his navy blue slacks, "Now it's your turn. Who wants to give me a situation?"

Instantly, the room was a sea of waving hands and rocklike faces glaring at Jennifer and Nora.

Jennifer's chest felt tight and her head felt light. Nora couldn't seem to catch her breath. Simultaneously, the girls slid down in their chairs and lowered their chins to their chests.

With Jennifer and Nora not speaking to one another, and no one else speaking to either one of them, the rest of the day was quiet. On the outside. On the inside, Jennifer's head buzzed with thought fragments: "The stupid notebook . . ." "Nora is so . . ." "All I was trying to do was . . ." "Everybody's so . . ."

Nora's mind, too, was filled with noise. She tried to apply the scientific method to the situation, but the problem seemed so broad in scope she had trouble formulating it. By the beginning of the last period of the day, however, she *had* managed to come up with a hypothesis: *Being mad at your best friend when everyone else is mad at you is not smart.* By the time the last bell rang, she realized it was more than a hypothesis; she'd had enough experience to call it a theory. As she walked — alone! — to her locker, she knew without a doubt it was a law — one that demanded action!

She hurried along the corridor, anxious to share this new insight with her friend, but Jennifer had already left the building.

"Nora? Is anything bothering you?" Jessica Ryan asked.

She'd just arrived home from work to find her daughter staring out the family room window.

Nora sighed heavily. "*Every*thing's bothering me," she responded as she let the beige homespun drape fall back against the window.

"Want to tell me about it?" Mrs. Ryan slipped off her coat, dropped it on the nearest chair, and sat down on the couch, adjusting a blue and red plaid pillow behind her back.

Nora sat beside her, took a deep breath and plunged in. She told her mother the whole story, putting the emphasis on her classmates' refusal to cooperate and their talking about her and Jennifer behind their backs. Because she could not yet deal with her growing sense of responsibility for the failure of the lunchhour meeting, she downplayed the parts of the story concerning the notebook and her quarrel with Jen.

Jessica Ryan listened attentively to the entire story without interrupting — her law experience made her a good listener — and then she summed up what Nora had told her, concluding, "First, I think you have to take a good look at your motives. Once you've satisfied yourself about those — "

"We're just trying to do a good job," Nora interrupted. "We want Cedar Groves to win."

"In that case, you can't worry about what people say about you." Mrs. Ryan pushed herself up off the couch and took her coat from the arm of the chair. She started for the door. "But remember," she said, "one can never change other people, only herself."

Nora sat for a long time, thinking about that.

Dear Diary, Jennifer wrote.

On days like this when she felt confused and alone, her blue diary was her best friend. It listened to her without making judgments, and it helped her sort through her conflicting feelings.

I learned something today: If a person is doing the right thing, and she is doing it the best way she knows how, she can't pay attention to what other people say. And as for that business about ethics: I don't think the means we were using to get to the end were all that bad. Actually, I don't think they were bad at all. Nora and I — we just . . . handled them wrong. Not wrong really — we just didn't go about things in the best way.

She sat back, thinking about Nora. Of all the bad things that happened today, what happened between her and Nora was the worst. She sighed as she continued:

Nora's mad at me. I hate it when we fight. It makes me feel all squishy inside. The awful part is she's probably right. Even if she did lose the notebook, it was mine. I should have been more careful with it.

She paused, her pen poised over her words. The only way she could have been more careful was not to have shown the notebook to Nora. It was *Nora* who lost it, she had no doubt about that; furthermore, it had been Nora's idea to try to make everybody perfect.

Actually, it's all as much Nora's fault as mine — MORE her fault than mine, she wrote. *I'm the one who should be mad. I AM MAD! Being mad at Nora makes me feel worse than having her mad at me.*

She read and reread the last line. She felt a rush of discovery. It was as if she had just decoded a secret message. Earlier today, she had rebuked herself for her inability to maintain a "simple friendship." Now, she thought, Friendship is never easy.

She wrote that down and then she rushed over to her telephone.

On her end, Nora had her hand on the phone, ready to pick it up to make a call, when it rang.

Chapter 11

"I was just going to call you!" Nora said when she realized it was Jennifer.

"Really?" Jennifer felt something ease inside her. She had thought this might be a difficult call, but Nora's welcoming tone dispelled her anxiety. She settled back against her eyelet-covered pillows and pulled her pink comforter up around her.

"I've been thinking about today," Nora went on.

"Wasn't it awful?" Jennifer broke in.

Nora groaned. "The worst day ever! I *hate* being mad at you. It makes me feel worse than anything. It's even worse than having you mad at me."

"Me, too," Jennifer said.

As different as they were, when it came right down to it, they felt very much alike on the important things.

"And that whole business in history!" Nora added.

"I've been thinking about that," Jennifer said. "Everybody acted like we were guilty of doing that — using bad means, but I don't think we were."

"I don't think so, either. And so I don't think we can worry about what other people say about us."

"Right," Jennifer concurred.

"The problem was we just . . . goofed. We handled everything the wrong way."

Jennifer laughed. "That's for sure."

"If you had talked to Jason privately like you said — "

"I didn't have the chance, Nora," Jennifer interrupted.

Detecting a note of irritation in her friend's voice, Nora said, "I know. I just meant it's too bad you didn't have the chance. Because that way, Jason probably wouldn't even have looked at the notebook. And he certainly wouldn't've read out everybody's names like he did."

Annoyance was forming inside Jennifer like an icicle, a drop at a time. Nora was still blaming her for what happened. "Oh, I think he would've anyway. Jason likes to cause trouble."

"I suppose you're right," Nora agreed. "The *real* problem was the notebook. I mean it was really dumb to put everything down like that." She was about to add, "We never should've done that," when Jennifer interrupted.

"You didn't think so when you told me to do it," she snapped and then she hung up, surprising them both.

Nora couldn't believe Jennifer had done that. For the first time all day, she had been willing to take equal blame for the disaster. Jennifer should have been happy to hear that. Instead, she was angry again. It was unfair. And juvenile! And she hadn't done anything to make Jennifer angry, either. Nora picked up the phone again. She just couldn't let Jennifer get away with this!

In her room, Jennifer pulled her fuzzy pink robe tight around her. Then, she marched to her desk and got her diary out of the top drawer. She reread the last line: *Friendship is never easy.* She crossed out the final two words and substituted *IMPOSSIBLE!!!*

The telephone rang.

Jennifer made no move to answer. If that was Nora wanting to apologize, she was too late.

It rang again.

On the other hand, Jennifer thought, she deserves to squirm a little.

She picked up the receiver on the fifth

ring, and held it to her ear without saying a word.

"Jen?" Nora asked into the silence. "Are you there? Because someone picked up the phone, so if you aren't there, there must be a ghost in your house."

That was so absurd it was funny. Jennifer laughed in spite of herself.

"Phew!" Nora said. "That's a relief. I don't know what I'd say to a ghost. Actually," she added, growing serious, "I don't even know what to say to you."

"You don't have to say anything," Jennifer told her. "It was all my fault." That was the second time she'd surprised herself tonight. She wondered if there'd ever be a time when she knew exactly what she thought before she said it or wrote it in her diary.

"No, Jen, it wasn't your fault," Nora protested.

"Was, too," Jennifer insisted. She dropped to the edge of her bed and reached for the denim bag on her night table.

After a pause, Nora chuckled. "I think we're fighting again," she said.

Jennifer twisted the pink telephone cord around her finger. "I don't want to do that," she said. "So have it your way: It was all your fault." Her tone was teasing.

Nora reached for her calico cat pillow.

"You don't have to go *that* far!" she responded lightly.

They both laughed.

Then, all the tension between them gone, Nora shifted comfortably into the business at hand, asking, "So what are we going to do, Jen?"

Jennifer fished inside her purse for her yellow notebook. "I haven't the slightest." It all seemed so hopeless. Under present conditions, Cedar Groves couldn't win. And no one was willing to make any changes.

"Maybe we should just act like nothing's happened," Nora suggested.

"They'd really talk about us then!" Jennifer said of their classmates. She cradled the phone between her ear and her shoulder to free both hands. Then she began tearing her lists into small pieces.

"I thought we decided we couldn't worry about what people said," Nora reminded her.

"I can *decide* all I want, Nora. That doesn't stop me from feeling bad about it."

Nora understood that completely. Often, her head and her heart seemed to be completely separate, one having no influence over the other. "But we have to ignore it, Jen, or we'll never be able to do our job," she said. "We have a responsibility."

"All we really have to do is show the

judges around," Jennifer reminded her as she crossed to the wastebasket beside her desk.

Nora began to pace the squares on the rug between her bed and bookcase. "But if we had something decent to show them, we'd have a better chance of winning."

Jennifer dropped the list fragments into her wastebasket. In the future, she would try not to make lists for everything. "There are the posters," she said.

"If Denise and Tracy haven't changed their minds about doing them."

"They wouldn't do that." That possibility had not occurred to Jennifer before. "Do you think they'd do that?"

"I don't know," Nora answered. She had to admit that if she were in their place, she might refuse to cooperate.

Jennifer mulled it over, deciding finally, "They won't quit. Tracy's always anxious to help, and Denise would consider it too juvenile to back out now."

"I hope you're right," Nora said. "Anyway, I think we should just . . . go ahead as we planned. We'll set up the dress code and hope some people decide to go by it. If we can get enough people doing it, everybody else'll do it, too."

"What should be put on it?"

"No jeans for one thing. Nice slacks or skirts for the girls."

Beside her bed, Jennifer picked up the yellow notebook. "And no far-out clothes, like Mia and Andy's," she added as she wrote: DRESS CODE.

"Or camouflage stuff."

"And no miniskirts."

"No miniskirts?" Nora said. She had been thinking of wearing her ice-washed denim mini. "I think minis are okay. I mean there're really in this year."

In or not, Jennifer didn't like them. Everyone said she could wear them well because she had such long, beautiful legs, but they made her uncomfortable. When she sat down, she felt as if she were all legs like the spider who sat down beside Miss Muffet. When she stood up, she felt even taller than she actually was. She realized, however, that everyone didn't feel as she about them. "Well, I suppose they're okay," she conceded.

"What'll we do about Jason?" Nora asked.

Jennifer sighed. "The only way we'll get that skateboard away from him is to take it," she said, meaning it merely as a comment, not a plan of action.

Imagining Jason's reaction to such an attempt, Nora laughed. "You can be in charge of that," she teased. Struck by a sudden thought, she added, "You know, this might not be as bad as we we think. I mean if no one cooperates, and we keep smiling no matter what, those judges'll think we're really terrific."

Jennifer put down her pencil. There was something to what Nora said. If they carried out their duties as hosts with a positive attitude, that would count for something. But was that enough? "What about everybody else?" she asked. She meant that the entire school was to be judged, not just herself and Nora.

Misunderstanding, Nora said, "We can't worry about what everybody else thinks or says or does, Jen. We just have to do the best we can. Considering what we have to work with, I think we're doing great!"

Chapter 12

"I don't think we should be so mean," Tracy Douglas said to those assembled on the school steps. Since their arrival this morning, everyone had been making snide comments about Nora and Jennifer. It made Tracy uncomfortable. She didn't like talking about people behind their backs. Finally, she had come to their rescue. "After all," she went on, "they're doing the best they can."

Susan snorted. "Yeah, right. Considering what they have to work with."

Thinking Susan was agreeing with her, Tracy nodded. "Trying to get this place in shape isn't easy," she said.

Tommy guffawed. "Nothing's easy for pea brains."

"You oughta know, Ryder," Jason put in.

Mitch laughed so hard he dropped the basketball he had been twirling on his forefinger.

Tommy grabbed the ball and tossed it. It bounced down the walk toward the street. Mitch told Tommy to get it. He refused. They scuffled. On the sidelines, Jason urged them on. The girls moved to another spot.

Her attention fixed on Tracy, Susan shook her head. "Sometimes I wonder what language you speak, Tracy."

Confused, Tracy frowned.

"Susan wasn't talking about school, Tracy," Lucy explained. "She meant that Nora and Jen aren't very smart. So their best isn't very good."

Tracy's eyes widened in disbelief. "You're wrong, Susan. Jen and Nora are very smart," she said, adding pointedly, "and nice, too, which is more than I can say for some people," before she turned her back.

Susan made a face and turned *her* back.

Jason sauntered over. "What're you two practicing for?" he asked them. "Living bookends?"

Denise joined the group. "Tracy," she said. "Gather everybody up. Maybe we can get the banner business settled before the bell rings."

"We're still doing that, huh?" Jason said.

Denise felt herself redden. She had thought about telling Nora and Jen to do the job themselves, but decided against it. Being older than most of her classmates, she felt a responsibility to set an example. If she backed out now, she'd be acting as immaturely as they. She turned her cool blue eyes on Jason. "Of course we're still doing it," she said. "Why wouldn't we be doing it?" Her tone said she hadn't even considered quitting.

Jason shrugged and held up his hands as if to fend off an attack. "Hey, listen, I'm on your side. I wouldn't back out, either. I mean just because somebody said I dressed all wrong . . ." He gave her the once-over. As always, Denise was perfectly dressed. Her lavender cropped sweater and beige slacks fit as though they had been made for her. Of course, it wouldn't really matter what she wore; she was so beautiful, she could wear a paper bag and people would still notice her. "They're right about one thing," he said, "You'll stand out all right." He meant that as a compliment.

Denise took it as an insult. "Jason Anthony, you are a creep!" she said, and, taking Tracy by the arm, she stalked off, leaving Jason murmuring, "What did I say?"

Nora and Jennifer met on the corner two blocks from school.

Saying, "I've got them!" Nora waved a batch of papers at Jennifer. "Sally let me use her computer."

"Let me see," Jennifer said.

Nora handed her a copy of the dress code. "I made one for each homeroom."

Jennifer scanned the notice. At the top, it said: WE ALL WANT CEDAR GROVES TO BE JUNIOR HIGH OF THE YEAR! "That's a good opening," she said.

"I thought we should start out with something positive," Nora responded.

"Something no one could argue with," Jennifer added, returning her attention to the list.

Our research has shown that other schools have dress codes.

"What research?" Jennifer asked.

"I wanted it to sound official," she said. "And there *are* schools with dress codes." Her tone was defensive.

"But why'd you have to say anything about research? It makes it sound like we did this big . . . study or something."

"I read an article about it once in *Seventeen* or some place," Nora responded. "That's research."

"I guess," Jennifer conceded. She glanced at the code. Nora had done a good job of setting up general rules without mentioning individual names.

"What do you think?" Nora asked anxiously. "Is it okay?"

Jennifer took one last look. There didn't seem to be anything here that would upset anyone. "It's great, Nora," she said.

Nora grinned. "I thought it was pretty good," she said. "And I figure if we're just tactful with everyone else — like Jason with his skateboard — I mean, if we don't come on too strong; if we just point out *reasons* they shouldn't do what they do — "

"Make things sound like suggestions instead of rules," Jennifer put in.

"Right," Nora said. "That way, they'll all cooperate."

Jennifer agreed. All was not lost. Everybody made mistakes. For all they knew, everyone had already forgotten about yesterday's meeting. "When are we going to put these up?" she asked, referring to the dress code notification.

"If we hurry, we can get around to all the homerooms before the bell rings."

Full of confidence, they ran the last half block, slowing only when they turned into the school walk. Heads turned and eyes glared at them as they made their way toward the stairs. Obviously, no one had forgotten about the meeting.

Jennifer could feel the confidence oozing out of her.

Nora, too, was experiencing doubt. "Act as if nothing's happened," she said to reassure herself as well as her friend. "Remember we're doing the right thing."

"*I'll* remember," Jennifer said, "but will *they*?"

Jason barreled toward them on his skateboard. "Hey, Jen," he called, "I hope you're not going to wear all those buttons Monday."

Jennifer looked down at her jacket. One side was full of pins: SAVE THE WHALES, EXTINCT IS FOREVER, TODAY IS THE FIRST DAY OF THE REST OF YOUR LIFE, THE CENTER OF LIFE IS IF . . . She was proud of her collection. "What's wrong with them?" she snapped.

Nora poked her. "Ignore him, Jen."

Jason sailed up beside Nora and took hold of her shirt tail, which was hanging below her jacket, "Tsk, tsk, Nora," he said. "Is this any way to dress?"

"It's supposed to be out," Nora said as she shifted her books to one arm and tucked her shirt up under her windbreaker with her free hand.

Jason circled the girls as he called to no one in particular. "Put Mann and Ryan on the list!" To them, he said, "How do you expect Cedar Groves to win when you two come to school looking like that?"

Nora stopped dead in her tracks. "Listen, you creep!" she bellowed.

"Nora!" Jennifer tugged at her friend's sleeve. "Come on. Don't pay any attention."

Nora ignored her. Her face red with anger, she sputtered, "*You're* the one who's going to spoil everything, Jason Anthony! You and that *stupid* skateboard!"

At her side, Jennifer wilted. Jason would never cooperate if Nora continued to attack him. "Come on, Nora," she urged. "The bell's going to ring."

Laughing, Jason raised a limp hand and skated away from the girls. "La-de-da," he taunted. "The hostess with the mostest."

Nora stood her ground. "If you think we're going to let you ride around on that stupid thing on Monday — !"

"*Let* me?!" Jason exploded. He executed an abrupt one-hundred-and-eighty-degree turn and headed right for Nora. "Let me?!"

As the gap between them closed, Nora's foot shot out to ward him off. At the same moment, Jason stopped short. Foot and board collided.

"Owww!" Nora howled.

Like launched rockets, her books flew out

of her arm toward Jason. He ducked, but the hard edge of her biology text clipped him on the shoulder.

"Owwwww!" he howled.

"Are you okay?" Jennifer asked Nora, who was dancing on one foot.

"I don't know," Nora answered. "My toe really hurts."

Jason moaned. "I think she broke my clavicle."

"Can you walk on it?" Jennifer asked.

"On my clavicle?" Jason responded. "I don't know. I've never tried."

Jennifer shot him a withering glance. "I'm not talking to you, Jason," she snapped.

Grimacing, Nora tried to put weight on her injured foot.

"Come on, Nora," Jennifer said. She gathered Nora's books and papers and stashed them under her arm. "I'll take you to the nurse's office."

"I'll come, too." Jason said.

Nora limped up the walk beside Jennifer. Bent toward his injured side, the opposite foot on the skateboard, Jason scooted along behind them.

Several of their classmates dashed down the stairs toward them, blocking the sidewalk.

"What happened?" Amy asked Nora.

Nora shook her head and groaned.

"She hit Jason with a book," Joan said.

"How do you know?" Lucy asked.

"I saw the whole thing," Joan answered.

"That's ridiculous," Amy said. "I was standing right next to you and I didn't see that."

"You weren't looking," Joan said.

"I was looking," Tracy put in. "It did look like Nora hit Jason with a book, but I'm sure she had a good reason."

"Jason plowed into Nora," Susan said, her voice full of authority. "*Then* she hit him with a book."

Nora groaned. Her toe was throbbing.

Jennifer waved her arm to make way. "Let us through."

"Right," Jason seconded.

The group parted to make a narrow corridor through which Nora limped. Jason moved along slowly, exaggerating his injury by drooping so far to one side, his hand scraped the walk.

Someone in the crowd made monkey sounds as he passed.

"That's it," Jason said, "kick a guy when he's down."

"Nora, maybe you should see the nurse," Jennifer said, following Nora into room 330.

Nora shook her head. "It's not broken."

"Are you sure?" Jennifer asked.

"Of course I'm sure." Nora's tone said:

"I'm going to be a doctor, remember; I should know a broken toe when I see one." Realizing how abrupt that sounded, she added, "It doesn't even hurt anymore."

"Okay. So, what are we doing in room 330?" Jennifer asked. Their homeroom was next door.

"Putting up the dress code," Nora said as she pulled the notices from her notebook. Giving Jennifer several sheets, she said, "You do the rooms across the hall. I'll do this side."

Jason wandered in, his skateboard under his arm.

At the sight of the board, Nora's temper flared. For her, the skateboard had become a symbol of all the things that would keep Cedar Groves from winning. Flashing him an angry look, she bellowed, "You're going to be sorry, Jason Anthony!"

His mouth curled in a lopsided grin as he turned amused eyes on her. "Who says?" His teasing tone infuriated Nora.

Taking two steps toward him, she said, "I says!" She paused. *I says?* she thought. It wasn't correct, she knew, but for several seconds, she was too befuddled to think clearly. "I mean —"

Jason chuckled smugly and wandered out.

"He is so — so — " Nora sputtered.

"Don't think about him, Nora," Jennifer

said. She edged toward the door. "Come on, let's finish putting up the notices."

Nora thrust her papers at Jennifer. "Here," she said, "you do it. I'll be right back." She marched out the door.

"Nora!" Jennifer called after her, but her friend was already around the corner out of sight.

The second bell rang.

Jennifer rushed next door to room 332.

Alone in the room, Mr. Mario looked up expectantly from the papers on his desk. "Is anyone with you?" he asked.

She looked behind her out into the hall. It was empty. "Guess not," she said.

He sighed. "I feel as though I'm the only one left on a sinking ship," he said.

Jennifer nodded solemnly. She felt exactly the same way. The more she tried to help, the more deserted and alone she felt. "Oh, don't worry," Jennifer assured him. "Everybody'll be here before it goes down." She felt herself redden. That hadn't come out right. And yet, she had to admit it expressed the situation accurately: Cedar Groves was the sinking ship; instead of helping to keep it afloat, the eighth grade was doing its best to scuttle it. "I mean — "

Mr. Mario laughed. "I wouldn't change a word," he said.

She asked his permission to put up the

dress code in the homerooms along this corridor while they waited for the others to arrive. He glanced over the notification, gave his approval, and sent her on her way.

She finished the job quickly and ducked into the girls' room.

"Nora?" she called. "Are you in here?" Silence.

Where are you? she wondered, trying to think like Nora, but it was hopeless. Nora didn't seem to be thinking this morning. She'd try the nurse's office. Maybe Nora had gone there after all.

Just as she was about to open the door on her way out, Nora dashed in. She stood against the door, hiding something behind her back. Her face was flushed with excitement and there was a wild look in her eyes.

"I did it!" she exclaimed. "I got it!"

"Did what? Got what?" Jennifer asked.

Nora slipped Jason's skateboard out from behind her back and held it up triumphantly.

Chapter 13

"I did it!" Nora repeated as she held up Jason's skateboard, bottom side facing out. Its four fluorescent green wheels stuck out like fists and its white skull decal, encircled by a green background, grinned at Jennifer. Her incredulous gaze slid from the board to Nora, who was grinning, too, and back again. "Nora! *What* are you doing with Jason's skateboard?!"

Nora dropped the board and hopped on for a ride to the opposite wall. "I took it," she said.

"Jason *let* you take this skateboard?"

Nora laughed. "Of course he didn't *let* me, Jen. I just took it." She pushed away from the wall and sailed back toward Jennifer. "He doesn't even know it's gone yet."

Jennifer was perplexed. The only time Jason let the board out of his sight was during classes when he stored it in his locker. She couldn't believe he'd be careless enough to leave it anywhere else. "Where'd you find it?"

Nora hopped off the board. "The usual place." She looked around the room for somewhere to hide it.

"His locker?" Jennifer said. "You took it from Jason's *locker*?"

Nora shrugged. "It was open."

Jennifer was too stunned to respond. Most eighth-graders left their lockers unlocked. It saved time. And it was understood that a person's locker was private. No one would think of opening a locker other than his own without the owner's permission.

Nora crossed to a storage cabinet. "How else was I going to get it?" She tried to wedge the board inside, but it was too shallow and the shelves prevented her from stashing it in an upright position.

"I thought we were going to talk to him — give him reasons why he shouldn't bring the skateboard on Monday," Jennifer said.

Nora closed the cabinet doors. "That'd never work."

"We didn't try," Jennifer reminded her.

Nora waved that fact away as though it were a pesky fly. "A waste of time, Jen. You know that. You said it yourself: 'The only way we'll get that skateboard away from him is to take it.' "

"Yeah, but I didn't mean we should do it," Jennifer said.

"We want to win, don't we?" Nora challenged.

"Sure, but — "

Hearing between Jen's words, Nora recognized her concern. "It's not like stealing or anything," she assured her friend. "I mean I'm not *keeping* the board. I didn't even take it for *me*; I took it for the class — for the whole *school*."

Jennifer knew that was true. Still, she felt there must be another way. And there was another problem: "What'll Jason do when he finds out?"

"He probably won't even miss it till school's over. We can be out of here before he is. Then there's the weekend and Monday. We'll give it back as soon as the judges leave."

"Why not wait until Monday morning to take it?" Jennifer asked.

"We won't have time, Jen. We have to go right to Mr. Donovan's office, remember?"

"But what if Jason's so mad, he decides not to hang the banners?"

Nora didn't have an answer to that question. She hadn't thought that far ahead. Actually, she hadn't thought much at all. She had been guided by her single-minded intention to get the skateboard. Now that she had it, she wasn't going to let any "what if's" spoil her sense of accomplishment. "Oh, Jen, you worry too much. The banners'll be up on Monday if we have to put them up ourselves."

Panic seeped into Jennifer's expression. "I can't come Sunday," she said. "There's open house at the animal shelter. I promised I'd be there."

"So we'll put them up Saturday."

"Denise said they're not making them till Saturday. Besides, I can't come then, either. I'm working at the shelter." Saturday morning was Jennifer's regular time at the animal shelter. This week, she'd probably work most of the day helping to get ready for Sunday.

"You mean you don't have any time over the weekend?"

"None."

"Then when are we going to clean off the glass casses in the hall?" Nora began to pace. "I can't do it all myself!"

Jennifer frowned. "The pictures," she repeated. She'd forgotten about them. "Didn't we agree to assign that job to somebody else?"

"Right, Jen," Nora said. "*We* agreed, but nobody else would. Don't you remember?" Before Jennifer had the chance to respond, she continued, "We can't think about that now; we have to figure out where to hide the skateboard."

Jennifer looked around. The room definitely had not been designed to hide skateboards.

The door opened and Mia rushed in. Nora quickly hid the board behind her back.

"How do I look?" Mia asked as she examined herself in the mirror. Two bandages crisscrossed in the center of her forehead. "I don't know why I didn't think of this before." She turned toward the girls.

"Are you hurt?" Jennifer asked.

Mia shook her head. "X for X, get it?" she said. "I think I'll buy some bandages — all different colors."

She breezed out of the room.

Imagining Mia with colored bandages all over, Jennifer flashed Nora an amused glance. "Can't you just see it? Bandages to match her hair," she commented, but Nora wasn't listening. Her attention was on the skateboard.

She set it against the corner wall behind a brown vinyl-cushioned chair. "Maybe we could just leave the board here — out in the open," she said. "Maybe nobody'd even notice."

Susan entered. "What's Jason's skateboard doing in here?" she demanded.

"We're keeping it for him," Nora answered.

Susan's eyes narrowed with suspicion. "Does *he* know that?"

Nora hoisted the board over the back of the chair. "Who gave *you* a police badge, Susan?" she asked. Then, saying, "Come on, Jen," she marched out of the room holding Jason's skateboard like a shield.

Susan's hands flew to her hips. "I'm going to tell!" she called as the door swung shut.

Following in Nora's tracks, Jennifer stopped abruptly outside the room. "There's Jason!"

Nora peeked over the board. Jason's red head was bobbing steadily toward them. She slipped into the rock room.

Jennifer made a move to follow, but she was too late. Jason had seen her.

"Hey, Jen," he said. He was actually smiling!

Jennifer averted her eyes. Still, the heat of his smile fell on her like a spotlight, exposing her guilt. Fortunately Jason didn't seem to notice her discomfort.

"Everyone was so late to homeroom, Mario said we should go right to first period," he told her.

"Okay. Thanks," she said and started along the hall.

Puzzled, he watched her go. "Wrong direction," he said, but she didn't respond.

When the coast was clear, Jennifer doubled back, meeting Nora at the rock room door.

"We did it!" Nora said.

The *we* made Jennifer uneasy. She knew Nora meant to share the credit, but she felt as though she were accepting the blame.

As first period passed without incident, Jennifer told herself she was overreacting. Typical. She always agonized over a decision before she made a move. Even after she'd taken action, she often wondered whether or not she had done the right thing. Left to her, Monday would have come and gone before she came up with a plan of action concerning Jason and his skateboard.

Nora, on the other hand, acted spontaneously. She was cool and quick-thinking in an emergency. That trait would help her later when she became a doctor, and it helped her now. This *was* an emergency, after all, and Nora had rushed in to correct it. Wishing she were more like her, Jennifer turned in her seat to watch her friend.

Across the aisle, Nora sat attentively, her eyes fixed on Mr. Rochester. Obviously, she wasn't giving the incident a second thought. And Jennifer resolved that she wouldn't either. What was done, was done. Now, she had to help keep Jason from finding the board.

Nora made a special effort to keep her eyes on Mr. Rochester. That way, it would look as though she were concentrating on the short story he was discussing with the class. Actually, she was mentally replaying this morning's events.

She had been so angry with Jason that she'd taken the board on impulse. Now, she wondered if she had done the right thing. Perhaps she was attaching too much significance to the board. It certainly wasn't the only problem at Cedar Groves. Would keeping Jason from it make any real difference in the judges' decision?

I should've told Jen what I was going to do, she thought. Jen had such a cool head. She would have insisted that Nora think beyond the moment. Sighing, she cast a glance toward her friend.

Jennifer smiled, a sign of her support.

Promising herself to try to be more like her friend in the future, Nora smiled in return.

"I'm sure glad I'm not them!" Lucy said of Jennifer and Nora.

She and some of the other girls were huddled at their usual cafeteria table discussing this morning's events. Everyone had been surprised that Nora and Jennifer hadn't even mentioned the notebook.

Denise said, "You'd think they would have apologized at least," with which everyone agreed except Tracy, who reminded them, "Nora broke her toe."

"That's right," Lucy put in. "They probably forgot all about the notebook when that happened."

"She didn't *break* it," Amy said.

"But she thought she did," Tracy argued. "Anyway, it must have hurt, the way she was limping."

Susan, who had been sitting silently at the head of the table, a smug expression on her face, said, "She was faking."

All eyes snapped challengingly in her direction.

"Well, she *was*," Susan said. "She never went to the nurse, did she?"

No one answered.

"And," Susan continued, "have you seen her limping since?"

The girls exchanged confused glances. Susan was right! What did it mean? They looked back to her expectantly.

Susan leaned forward. "And *why* was she faking? To distract everybody so she could come inside and steal Jason's skate-board!" There. It was out. She sat back and waited for her audience's reaction.

There was a long pause. Then, Lucy laughed. "You've got to be kidding!"

Susan's shrug said "Don't believe me. I couldn't care less."

"Why would she do *that*?" Amy asked.

"*How* could she do that?" Denise asked.

Susan shrugged again. "She did it — that's all I know."

Just then, Jason marched into the cafe-teria. His eyes darted around the room. In his camouflage pants and T-shirt, he was a commando ready for action. He spotted the girls and stomped toward them.

"Where are Ryan and Mann?" he de-manded. His eyes sparked. His freckles seemed to have run together, making his face one reddish flush. His red hair shot in all directions like fiery flames.

Mumbling their ignorance — they had no idea where Nora and Jennifer were and wouldn't have said if they did — the girls tried to ignore him. But it was impossible.

Then Susan spoke up. "Is something wrong, Jason?" she asked, knowing the answer.

"My skateboard's missing," he snapped.

Still unwilling to accept Susan's ex-planation, Lucy asked, "Where'd you leave it?"

"In my locker," he answered.

Dumbfounded, the girls said, "Your locker?" in unison.

Susan glanced around the table. Her expression said, "I told you so."

Jason stalked off after his prey.

"I'd sure hate to be them," Lucy repeated.

After gym class, Jennifer and Nora stopped in the office to get permission for the banner committee to be in school on Sunday. Then, they hurried toward the cafeteria.

At the door to the rock room, Nora said, "We'd better check to see if Jason's board's still here."

Sometimes, a teacher used the room to give a makeup test. She was afraid it might have been discovered.

Jennifer followed her into the room. The luminous skull on the bottom of the deck grinned at them through the dark.

Directing Jennifer to close the door, Nora snapped on the light. "Right where I put it," she said.

"Do you think we should leave it here?" Jennifer asked. Once Jason discovered it missing, he'd probably look here.

"We'll move it later," Nora said. "Let's go eat now."

Uncomfortable under the unrelenting

stare of the skull, Jennifer asked, "Could you turn it around at least?"

Nora complied and then the girls headed out of the room. They ducked back inside when they caught a glimpse of Jason turning the corner near the cafeteria.

"Do you suppose he knows?" Jennifer whispered.

Nora shook her head. "He never goes to his locker until after school," she said confidently.

"Where've you two been?" Susan asked when Nora and Jennifer sat down.

"Getting permission for the weekend," Nora said. "It's all set," she told Denise and Tracy. "Jen can't help, but I'll be here."

Denise bristled. She'd been given the responsibility of heading the committee for the banners and now it looked as though Nora intended to take over. "Don't you trust me or what?" she asked.

Nora was surprised at her reaction. She felt as though it was her duty to follow up. "Of course I trust you, Denise. Why wouldn't I trust you?"

"We just don't need anyone . . . looking over our shoulders," Denise said.

Obviously offended, Nora said, "I just thought I could help."

Denise softened. Maybe Nora's intentions were good. "We can handle it," she said. "It's our job, and we'll do it. Right, Trace?"

Tracy hadn't been listening. She was thinking about Jason and his skateboard. When Denise addressed her, she automatically expressed what was on her mind. "Nora, why'd you take Jason's skateboard?"

Nora glared at Susan. Susan-the-gossip had been busy. "What *else* could we do?" she said. "We couldn't let him spoil everything on Monday." Her sweeping glance included everyone, as though each had a part in this.

"*We*?" Lucy said.

"*We!*" Denise said. "I don't remember anyone asking my opinion."

"Right, Nora," Amy put in. "You and Jen could've talked to us about this."

"We could've taken a vote or something," Lucy added.

Nora shot to her feet. "The judges'll be here on Monday!" she sputtered. "We couldn't waste time being . . . democratic!"

Chapter 14

"Come on, Jen," Nora said. "Let's find someone who has some school spirit. Someone who's interested in Cedar Groves Junior High and not just themselves." She stormed off, leaving everyone openmouthed behind her.

Jennifer hung back. She had sat silently through Nora's outburst feeling more and more uncomfortable. Now, she felt compelled to apologize for her friend. "Don't mind her," she said. "She's really nervous about Monday. She just wants everything to be perfect."

"She should start with herself," Lucy said.

In the center of the room, Nora turned on her heel. "Jen!" she called.

Sighing, Jennifer dutifully obeyed the command.

"Hurry," Nora prompted her. "We have

to move the board. Susan and her big mouth," she added to explain the urgency. Susan had surely told Jason or someone else who had told him. He was probably already tearing the place apart in search of his beloved skateboard.

Referring to their friends, Jennifer asked, "Don't you think you were kind of hard on them?"

"You heard them, Jen," Nora snapped. "They criticize everything we do."

"They were just surprised you'd — we'd — taken Jason's board like that," Jennifer explained. First she'd apologized for Nora, and now she was apologizing for the other girls. How'd I get in the middle? she wondered.

Nora stopped abruptly. Her determined expression changed into one of dismay.

Jennifer followed her gaze. Rocketing toward them from the opposite end of the hall was Jason on his skateboard! Relief flooded her. Now, there'd be no need to find hiding places. No chance of a messy confrontation. No pangs of conscience. Without realizing it, she smiled.

At first, Nora was confused by Jen's reaction. Then, she, too, smiled. "That's it, Jen," she said. "Smile! Keep smiling no matter what!" It had been her suggestion — a way to captivate the judges in front of their uncooperative classmates. They were wise to begin practicing now. Besides, what else could they do?

Heading right for them, Jason smiled, too. Then, as Nora and Jennifer jumped aside to let him through, he thumbed his nose at them.

Jennifer expected the afternoon to be disastrous, but, instead, it was calm and pleasant. Everyone was especially polite to her and Nora. In view of the events of the last few days, it was puzzling. And unsettling.

Nora tried to see the change as a positive one. Perhaps people were finally beginning to realize that she and Jen had the school's best interests at heart. A part of her, however, remained unconvinced.

"You going to Temptations?" Tracy asked Nora and Jen after school.

Denise gave her a poke. Their committee meeting, originally scheduled for the resource center, had been moved to Temptations, the local ice cream parlor, at the last minute for a reason: less chance of running into Jennifer and Nora.

Already upset with the two girls' leadership, the class had gone berserk over the skateboard business. Separating Jason and the board was not the issue — at some time during the past several weeks, everyone had wanted to do that — but taking it from his locker was something else again. A blatant invasion of privacy, it threatened them all. The episode had so disoriented them that they walked through the afternoon like sleepwalkers.

"What's happening at Temptations, Trace?" Nora asked as she slammed her locker door shut.

Flashing Tracy a warning glance, Denise put in quickly, "Nothing."

The confusion in Tracy's eyes cleared up suddenly. "Oh, yeah. Right. Nothing's happening at Temptations."

"Then why'd you ask?" Nora said.

Tracy looked helplessly at Denise, who came to her rescue with a casual shrug and, "She just wondered if you were going."

Tracy imitated the shrug. "I just wondered if you were going," she repeated.

"It's too cold for ice cream," Jennifer said. "Besides, I haven't much time."

Tracy beamed. "Good," she said.

Denise gave her another poke.

"I've decided to skip the pictures," Nora said on the way home, choosing to avoid the subject most on her mind: the conversation they'd just had with Denise and

Tracy. "I'll never have time to wash all the glass myself, and if some are clean, the dirty ones'll look even dirtier."

Jennifer only half-heard. "Good idea," she said, her mind on Tracy's strange behavior. "What do you suppose that was all about?"

"You mean Tracy and Denise?" Nora shook her head. "I haven't a clue," she said. "It's probably not worth thinking about."

Jennifer turned to look at her friend. "But something's going on for sure."

"It probably had something to do with the way everyone was acting all afternoon," Nora said. "All that politeness — sickening."

"You noticed that, too?" Jennifer had begun to think she was imagining things. "Even Jason! I expected him to say something. He had to be really angry, but he never said a word." Reluctant to voice her next thought, she paused briefly. "It was almost as if they were . . . afraid of us or something."

"Exactly," Nora murmured. "And then all that business about Temptations. . . . You're right, Jen: Something's definitely up."

They walked along in silence, each trying to unravel the mystery.

Finally, Nora said, "The only thing I

know for sure is that the more perfect we try to make everything, the worse it gets."

Because Jennifer was busy all weekend, Nora had plenty of time to think about the week's activities. Try as she might, she could not erase the feeling that much of what had happened was her fault. She had taken her responsibility seriously — a good quality. Now, though, she felt as if she might have taken it too seriously. Perhaps she had tried to accomplish too much. Because she had been so negative for the past several weeks, she had looked upon this assignment as a chance to redeem herself. She would show her classmates how much school spirit she had. And, she admitted, how little they had.

By Sunday, Nora knew she had to stop in at school whether Denise and her committee wanted her there or not. It was her job to encourage their efforts. And she owed it to them, to herself, to apologize.

She met Brad and Steve at the school's front door.

Steve said, "What're you doing here?"

Now that she was actually here, she wasn't quite sure how to answer. Her confidence and resolve were shaky this morning, and, walking to school, she was aware of a growing sense of apprehension. Half-way there, she had considered going home, mission incomplete. Now, basking in Brad's beautiful, broad smile, she was glad she hadn't.

Saying, "I could ask you the same thing," she grinned at Brad as he rushed to hold the door for her.

"My committee's setting tables in the faculty lunchroom," Steve answered as he trailed her inside.

"The judges aren't eating in the cafeteria?" Nora had assumed they'd have lunch with her and Jen.

"No," Steve told her. "They're eating with the teachers."

That was a relief. At least she and Jen would have lunch period to themselves.

"Even the menu is different," Steve continued.

She laughed. "Good thing."

"Right," Brad put in. "We wouldn't want to poison them."

They stopped in the main hall before the bulletin board, where the banner committee had already completed its work. A collage of captioned photos depicting various aspects of Cedar Groves Junior High life filled the board. Every class was represented, along with every activity. A banner with a sketch of the school in one corner was placed along the top of the board. It read:

WELCOME TO CEDAR GROVES JUNIOR HIGH —
THE SCHOOL WITH SPIRIT.

"Awesome!" Steve and Brad commented simultaneously.

For her part, Nora was speechless. She had never expected anything like this. Her confidence sprang to life as though it were a dry plant in a warm, life-giving rain.

Barely able to contain her delight, she hurried on toward the auditorium. Self-satisfaction welled up in her. She wished Jennifer could be here to share in the triumph. Perhaps they had made a few mistakes along the way, but, nonetheless, their efforts had not been in vain. Certainly, with results like this, they had no reason to apologize for anything.

The sound of excited voices from the gym grew louder as her steps quickened. She ran down the hall, stopping with breathless anticipation at the open doors.

Inside, people sat on the floor working over long, wide strips of paper; others held up finished work; some affixed banners along the side of the room. Everyone was smiling.

CEDAR GROVES HAS HEART, she read, and CEDAR GROVES, A GOOD PLACE TO GROW.

She leaped into the gym, arms raised like a cheerleader. "We are the best!" she shouted.

Instantly, the smiles froze, the room quieted. Everyone stopped working and turned to look at her.

"Let's hear it for us!" she cried. "Hip, hip hooray!" — No one moved. They continued to stare at her in stony silence. "Hip, hip. . . . " Her voice cracked and trailed off.

Disquieting murmurs rippled through the room.

Nora cleared her throat. She drew her head into her shoulders like a wary bird. "Hi, everybody," she said weakly.

Denise came forward. "Hi, Nora," she said. "We didn't expect you."

"Yeah, well, I just thought I'd stop in to see how you're doing."

"We're doing okay," Denise said. Then, indicating the group with a sweep of her hand, she added, "It's a great group."

"You're sure doing a good job," Nora responded. "The bulletin board is terrific. Are you almost finished?" She meant that as a sign of her interest, but those who heard it took it as criticism.

"We'll be finished on time," Denise said, her words clipped. "You don't have to worry about that."

"Oh, I wasn't worried," Nora put in quickly. "I mean, it looks like you're almost finished already."

"We'll have a few things to do tomorrow morning," Denise said, "but otherwise —"

Jason cruised up on his skateboard. "We're saving the best for last," he said.

Missing the mischievous twinkle in his eye, Nora smiled. "I can't wait."

Jason chuckled. He glanced around at the people who had drifted over in his wake. "Neither can we," he said.

Everyone looked at her, waiting for her reply.

She had no idea what she was expected to say. "I think we have a good chance of winning," she offered, but it didn't seem to satisfy them. Finally, she came up with, "Like they say, 'Winning isn't everything; it's the only thing.' "

There was a long pause. Amy was the first to break the silence. " 'It doesn't matter whether you win or lose,' " she quoted. " 'It's how you play the game.' "

"Well, yes," Nora conceded, "there's that, too." She edged toward the door. "I guess you don't need me," she said. "I'd uh, better be going."

As she turned and left the gym, everyone scurried back to work, bubbling with excitement as if they'd suddenly been released from captivity.

"Jen, you won't believe your eyes!" Nora told Jen later.

Jennifer twisted her phone cord around her finger. One part of her was relieved to hear that the class had finally decided to cooperate, while another part felt unready to accept at face value this abrupt change. They're up to something, she thought, immediately dismissing it. "We have Denise to thank," she said. "She's a really good leader."

"We have *ourselves* to thank, Jen," Nora said. "After all, we chose Denise."

"At least we did one good thing."

"You're too hard on yourself," Nora told her. "You did lots to make this work. We both did."

"What about Jason?"

"No biggie," Nora said. "He didn't say a word."

"That's what scares me," Jennifer admitted. "I mean it isn't like Jason to let something like that go."

"Obviously, he's 'put aside individual concerns for the greater good,' " Nora said.

Jennifer couldn't believe her ears. "Who said that?" she asked.

Nora giggled. "I did. Didn't you hear me?"

"I mean who *first*; who *said* it first?"

"If some people did their homework . . ." Nora teased. The quote had come from the history unit due tomorrow.

"I've been busy," Jennifer said.

"How'd it go?"

"Pretty good. Some of the visitors decided to adopt animals and lots made donations. I kept thinking about tomorrow, though, so I didn't enjoy it as much as I would've another time."

Nora opened her closet door. "What're you wearing?"

Jennifer sighed and leaned back against her pillows. "I don't know. I keep deciding and then changing my mind. I wish I could be like you: more . . . decisive."

"I can't make up my mind, either."

Jennifer sat up. "I thought you were wearing the denim mini."

Nora closed her closet door. "I don't think so. It's too . . . casual."

Twirling her long hair around her finger, Jennifer said, "I am so nervous about all this."

"Don't think of it as *nervous*, Jen. Be positive. Think of it as *excited*."

Jennifer giggled. "In that case, I am *really* excited."

Nora giggled, too. "You don't even know what excitement is! Just wait till tomorrow! I'm telling you, Jen, you will not believe your eyes!"

Chapter 15

"You were right, Nora," Jennifer said next morning as the two girls approached the school. "I don't believe my eyes."

At her side, Nora gaped at the scene. "This isn't exactly what I meant," she said.

A long line of people, with Jason in the lead, moved up and down on the walk at the foot of the front stairs. They were carrying signs and chanting. And they moved in a peculiar way — as though they were on conveyor belts.

"Are they on rollers or what?" Jennifer asked.

"Skateboards!" Nora exclaimed. "They are practically all on skateboards!"

As the girls approached slowly, silently, the chant swelled: *"FREEDOM! FREEDOM! FREEDOM!"* And the signs came into focus: *ON STRIKE AGAINST TYRANNY; DOWN WITH DICTATORS;*

CHOICE IS CHOICE; LEADERS SHOULD LEAD, NOT RULE.

Someone spotted Jennifer and Nora. The line broke. Everyone came toward them, some skating, some running.

Nora nudged Jennifer. "Remember," she said between her teeth, "keep smiling."

Jennifer tried to comply, but her face seemed to be frozen in place.

The line re-formed on either side of them as the chant reached a deafening crescendo.

Her lips locked in a vacant grin, Nora took hold of Jennifer's jacket sleeve and urged her on. Flanked by chanting class-mates, they made their way to the stairs, where those on boards halted. A few others ascended along with them to the double doors.

There, someone shouted, "They're goin' in!"

That was enough to stop everyone. The bell hadn't rung. They were not so intent on revenge that they'd venture inside on a school morning before it was absolutely necessary.

"Saved by the bell," Nora said ironically as the two girls slipped inside.

"Too bad we can't keep it from ringing all day," Jennifer commented.

Ahead, near the main bulletin board out-side his office, Mr. Donovan huddled with three strangers. *The judges!*

Jennifer smoothed the front of her beige corduroy skirt. "Do I look all right?" she asked, panic in her voice.

"Great," Nora said without looking. "How about me?" She had decided on Sally's oxford cloth blouse and her own straight, knee-length taupe skirt at the last minute. Now, the collar felt too tight and the waistband itched.

Mr. Donovan saw them. "Here they are now," he said.

The two men and the woman turned their attention toward the girls. The three of them looked amazingly alike. All wore three-piece suits, glasses, and stern expressions. The only real difference was that both men were balding and the woman wasn't.

Mr. Donovan stepped forward. "Nora, Jennifer, I'd like you to meet Mr. Stillwell, state assistant superintendent" — Mr. Stillwell nodded — "Mr. Elisius — "

"Rhymes with delicious," the man put in.

" — chairperson of the state's Special Curriculum Commission." Mr. Donovan continued. "And, last, but certainly not least," — he smiled at the woman — "our state school board president, Ms. Lombardi."

Smiling broadly, the woman extended her hand.

Both girls moved to shake it at the same time. Unruffled, Ms. Lombardi closed their two hands in both of hers. "We've been admiring this wonderful bulletin board," she said.

"Quite a job," Mr. Elisius commented. "We understand it was done without adult supervision."

"Yes, sir," Nora said.

Nodding, Mr. Stillwell said, "Hmmm," as though he were noting her response on some invisible list.

Then nobody said anything.

Mr. Donovan cleared his throat. "Well, girls," he said, "I'm sure our guests have had enough of me."

The judges chuckled politely.

"We've been closeted in my office since seven o'clock this morning, taking care of the paper work," the principal explained.

Nora and Jennifer exchanged relieved glances. That meant they hadn't seen the picket line outside! Lady Luck was with them. Now, if she'd only stay awhile. . . .

"It's all yours," Mr. Donovan went on. "I'm sure you will be excellent guides." To Jennifer and Nora his words sounded as much like a warning as they did a vote of confidence.

"Is there a schedule or something?" Jennifer asked.

"Your usual schedule is fine," Mr. Donovan answered. "If there's anything our guests are particularly interested in seeing, they'll tell you." His eyes twinkled. "And don't worry about being on time for classes. Today, you have my permission to be late."

What we need is permission not to show up at all, Nora thought. She said, "Thank you, Mr. Donovan."

He gave them a go-to-it smile. Then he shook hands all around and retreated into his office.

"Is there anything you'd like to see now?" Nora asked.

Mr. Elisius looked at the others to be sure they had no requests before saying, "Whatever you usually do now is fine. We'll just follow along."

"Usually, we don't come inside before the bell rings," Jennifer said.

"That's fine," Mr. Elisius said. "We'd be happy to get a breath of fresh air." He turned toward the front doors.

"Oh, no!" Nora said. "We can't go out *there*!"

They all looked at her inquiringly.

"What Nora means is . . . the bell's going to ring any minute," Jennifer said. "There's no time."

"What do you do after the bell rings?" Ms. Lombardi asked.

"We — uh —" Jennifer couldn't remember.

" — go to our lockers," Nora said. She back-stepped in that direction.

"Lead on," Mr. Elisius said.

"Just forget we're here," Ms. Lombardi added.

Thinking, We'd rather forget *we're* here! the girls led the silent parade through the front hall, where the worn spots in the tile seemed to jump out at them like gigantic black holes ready to pull them in.

Nora directed the judges' attention upward. "You'll notice this hall is lined with class pictures going back to the very first one," she said.

Mr. Stillwell nodded. "Hmmm," he said, moving to take a closer look.

Horrified, Jennifer saw the words CLEAN ME written in the dust on the glass of several. She darted to the opposite side of the hall. "Over here," she directed, "are windows overlooking the front lawn. In the spring, it's very green. Of course at this time of year —" She glanced outside. Jason and the others were still out there waving signs. She turned on her heel. " — it's . . . pretty yucky." She moved swiftly down the hall.

Mr. Elisius cocked his head toward the windows. "Do I hear chanting?" he asked.

Neither girl knew how to reply. Fortunately, Ms. Lombardi answered for them, saying, "Cheerleading practice."

Mr. Stillwell accepted that with his usual, "Hmmm."

As they turned the corner toward the lockers, they spotted Mia and Andy coming toward them. Andy wore his black tails. An inch of white sports socks was visible between the hem of the black pants and his red and white Air Jordans. His purple and orange spiked hair matched Mia's. She wore her skin-tight leopard leotard and tights topped with her zebra-striped big shirt. The green cabbage rose was tucked into one black combat boot. A large safety pin dangled from each ear.

Nora did an abrupt about-face. "On second thought, we don't need to go to our lockers." She looked to Jen for confirmation.

"You've got a point there," Jennifer responded. "Lockers are lockers." Then, just as she was about to change direction, Mia and Andy disappeared around the corner at the opposite end of the bank of lockers. "But then again," she said, "we might need some books for class."

"Books?" Nora said as though it were a foreign word. She glanced over her shoulder. The coast was clear. "Books! Oh, right," she said. "I forgot." She changed directions again.

"Who were those . . . people?" Ms. Lombardi asked.

"People?" Jennifer said, feigning innocence.

"The ones with the strange . . . clothes," Ms. Lombardi said.

Nora laughed nervously. "Oh, them," she said. "They're not *people*; they're . . ." Unable to think of an appropriate word, she shrugged.

"Seventh-graders," Jennifer volunteered.

All three judges nodded sagely.

At their lockers, Mr. Elisius noticed Jennifer's SAVE THE WHALES poster. "Nice to know young people are interested in the environment," he said.

"Jennifer's interested in all kinds of projects," Nora told him. "She works at an animal shelter and helps out at the Cedar Groves Nursing Home, too."

Ms. Lombardi beamed. "How do you handle so much?"

Blushing, Jennifer shrugged modestly.

"She's very organized," Nora answered for her.

Jennifer opened her locker. Yellow notebooks cascaded out, landing on the floor with one thump after another. Small yellow notebooks. Large yellow notebooks. One subject yellow notebooks. Three-subject yellow notebooks. Five-subject yellow notebooks. Plain yellow notebooks. Fancy yellow notebooks. Everywhere — YELLOW NOTEBOOKS!

Six eyebrows bounced up over three pairs of glasses.

Jennifer stood stockstill staring at the yellow flood engulfing her ankles.

"Jen believes in taking lots of notes," Nora explained. Then, taking a deep breath, she flung open *her* locker, jumping aside to avoid whatever might fall out.

Nothing did. Instead, a blue dragon spit fire at her from the deck of a skateboard — the only thing in the locker. Its taunting, glassy eyes seemed to be saying "Gotcha!" She slammed the door shut.

"Now that's what I call an endangered species," Mr. Elisius said, referring to the dragon.

Ms. Lombardi laughed.

Mr. Stillwell said, "Hmmm."

The bell rang.

"Keep smiling," Nora hissed to Jennifer as they began the trek toward homeroom.

"I think I forgot how," Jennifer hissed back.

Coming toward them, Tommy, Mitch, and Marc whipped out combs and ran them through their hair.

Nora and Jennifer made a sharp turn.

"All the seventh grade homerooms are in this hall," Nora said as she picked up her pace.

Quick-stepping beside her, Jennifer added, "We thought you'd like to see them."

Ahead, a red-topped blur crossed the corridor. Jason on his skateboard!

Nora did an about-face, colliding with Mr. Elisius. She maneuvered around him and tore back along the corridor.

At the opposite end, another wraithlike figure zipped by.

Jennifer turned into the nearest open room. A closet! The others piled up behind her. She held up a push broom. "We have . . . very good . . ." Her voice trailed off. She looked at the broom as though she'd never seen one before.

"Brooms," Ms. Lombardi said.

"Mops, too," Nora put in. "Show them a mop, Jen."

Jennifer held up a mop.

"We might not have a TV studio like Hubbard Woods," Nora went on, "but we have the essentials."

Homeroom was in progress by the time Nora and Jennifer ushered in their breathless guests.

Mr. Mario greeted them at the door.

Then, turning to the girls, he said, "Will you do the honors?"

Puzzled, the girls looked at one another and then back at Mr. Mario, who said, "Introduce our guests to the class."

"Oh, sure," Nora said. She stepped forward. "Everybody, we'd like you to meet — " She glanced over her shoulder. Mr. Elisius stood closest to her. She would introduce him first. " — Mr. Delicious." Instantly, a stricken expression swept over her face. That wasn't right; but what was?

Snickers rippled through the room.

Jennifer sprang to the rescue. "What Nora means is 'it *rhymes* with delicious.' " She smiled at the man as if to say, You see, I was listening, before continuing, "It's Mr. Elisius." She pronounced it *E-li-see-us*.

The class roared. Fortunately, no one enjoyed the mix-up more than Mr. Elisius.

After what they'd been through, Nora and Jennifer dreaded morning classes, but they were surprised and relieved to find their fears unfounded. Electric with excitement, the air seemed to charge teachers and students alike with enthusiasm. And if it took somewhat longer than usual to settle down, the energy level remained high throughout each period so that more was accomplished in a shorter time.

By lunchtime, the girls were feeling relaxed and confident. Everything that could go wrong had gone wrong. There was nothing more to worry about.

"The faculty lunchroom is through the cafeteria," Jennifer said as she and the others threaded their way through the rushing stream of hungry students.

"There's a special menu and everything," Nora said.

"One of the eighth-graders — Steve Crowley" — Jennifer put special emphasis on the name — "was in charge."

"Brad Hartley helped," Nora added.

The judges seemed duly impressed.

Moved by a kind of upbeat, interior music, Nora and Jennifer waltzed into the cafeteria. There, the music died.

Strung up over the gleaming stainless steel food tables where it could not be missed was the biggest banner of them all. It screamed its message:

NORA RYAN EATS WORMS

The first to recover, Jennifer twirled to face the judges. "Right this way," she said and, averting her eyes as though she thought if she couldn't see the banner, the judges couldn't either, she led the way. Nora remained transfixed to the spot.

At the faculty lunchroom door, Ms. Lombardi asked, "Does she really eat . . . worms?"

Without missing a beat, Jennifer answered, "Nora's very interested in health food."

A change in the afternoon's schedule was announced toward the end of lunch period. American history classes would be combined and meet in the resource center. Although Mr. Carpenter and Mr. Robards had covered special material in this way before, they had always made arrangements far in advance. This sudden alteration — especially today — was puzzling.

Everyone arrived early for history, bubbling with curiosity.

Jennifer and Nora were the last to enter, along with the judges, who murmured approval over the student eagerness.

When everyone had found a place, Mr. Carpenter said, "We have been studying political process for several weeks now, and certain . . . events. . . ."

Chuckling, Mr. Robards put in, "Certain *current* events."

Mr. Carpenter smiled at his colleague. "*Timely* events," he said. "These . . . events of the day have prompted us to hold this joint session for the purpose of summarizing what we have learned thus far."

Alternately, the two teachers reviewed the highlights of the last several lessons, paying particular attention to vocabulary: *Political ethics; Totalitarianism; Socialism; Democracy.*

"In a democracy," Mr. Robards said, "room must be made for the expression of dissenting opinion."

"How is this accomplished?" Mr. Carpenter asked.

Several people called out answers: "Through a free press." "*All* the media." "Demonstrations." "Voting."

Mr. Carpenter held up his hands. "Not so fast. Let's take these things one at a time. Voting. In many places people vote, but they are given only one candidate."

"In a democracy, you have to have choices," Tommy said.

"That's why we have the party system," Joan said. "In the United States, the two main parties are the Democrats and the Republicans."

Tracy waved her hand. "Nora says it's a waste of time to be a Democrat."

A surprised murmur swept through the room.

Nora shot to her feet. "I never said any such thing!"

Mr. Robards studied her. "Would you like to tell us what you *did* say?"

Her face went red-hot and her palms got clammy. "I'm not sure exactly." She glanced furtively toward the judges as she tried to reconstruct the earlier conversation. It had something to do with them, with getting ready for their visit. "I said — I *think* I said — that sometimes being democratic — listening to everybody's opinion, taking votes and all that — well, there isn't always time to do that."

Nora heard a soft, "Boo!"

Mr. Robards nodded. "Perhaps we have to make the time," he suggested. "Because if we don't, what might be the result?"

The entire morning — the whole last week! — flashed before Nora's eyes. "Well, people could . . . refuse to cooperate?" she offered tentatively.

Mr. Carpenter said, "They might even . . . ?" He looked around the room expectantly.

"Revolt!" Jason exclaimed.

"Revolution. Anarchy." Mr. Robards said. "Reasons?"

Heads swiveled to glare at Nora and Jennifer as all the separate voices rose as one: "Dictators!"

Chapter 16

Although Jennifer and Nora felt it never would, the school day ended. Finally.

They escorted the judges back to the office, where Mr. Donovan was waiting for them. "How did it go?" he asked.

"Interesting," Ms. Lombardi responded.

"Enlightening," Mr. Elisius replied.

"It has been a most interesting and enlightening day," Mr. Stillwell summed up.

Mr. Donovan smiled. "Cedar Groves is an interesting, enlightening place," he said.

Everyone nodded.

"How long before results are announced?" the principal asked.

Mr. Stillwell looked from one judge to the other. Then, as if he had just counted a silent vote, he said, "Soon. Very soon."

"We've seen all the other schools," Mr. Elisius said.

"Cedar Groves was the last," Ms. Lombardi added.

Chuckling, Mr. Donovan said, "And most memorable."

Everyone smiled politely.

The girls accepted the judges' thanks, said their good-byes, and were released. At last!

Side by side, they trudged silently through the empty halls to the front door, unaware of the dusty beams that lit the way.

They were two blocks away before Jennifer broke the silence. "I think I'm going to be sick," she said.

"I already am!" Nora said.

"Sick enough to stay home tomorrow?"

"Sick enough to stay home till summer."

They lapsed into silence. Then, Nora began to giggle.

"What's so funny?" Jennifer asked, beginning to giggle, too.

"Those notebooks!"

"If I ever see another yellow thing . . . !"

"The look on your face!"

"You should've seen yours — that skateboard!"

They doubled over with laughter.

"Nora!" Jennifer said, trying to regain control. "We shouldn't be laughing like this. Cedar Groves just lost and we're — "

A laugh swept away the last word.

"Who knows?" Nora dug a tissue out of her pocket. "We might win!" She dabbed at her eyes. "Remember what the judges said: 'Interesting. Enlightening.'"

"That's for sure! They think you — you — " Jennifer couldn't get it out. She tried again. "I — I told them you — They think you eat worms!"

"Why not?" Nora sputtered. "They're full of protein!" She remembered something else. "Mia! Andy! Did you see the looks on the judges' faces when they came into English?" She tried to imitate their astonished expressions but her heart wasn't in it. "We said they were in seventh grade!"

Jennifer understood. "And they turned up in all our classes!"

They laughed until there wasn't a laugh left in them.

"I'll bet Hubbard Woods wasn't nearly as 'enlightening,'" Nora said.

That reminded Jennifer of brooms and mops. "Hubbard Woods," she scoffed. "I mean tell me: Do they have essentials like we have essentials?"

"That's very funny," Nora said. "I'd laugh, only my ribs hurt."

"It's my jaw that hurts," Jennifer said. After a while, she asked, "So are we going to school tomorrow or what?"

Nora thought about it. "I guess we have to face the music."

Jennifer nodded. "Even if it is the wrong tune."

Jennifer and Nora stuck especially close together as they approached school next morning. Geared for The Attack, they were relieved to discover The Silent Treatment was the order of the day. They pretended not to notice and smiled through one long, quiet period after another.

"After all," they reminded one another, "we did the best we could."

At the end of the day, though, Jennifer confessed, "I wish somebody'd yell at us or something."

"They will," Nora predicted. "Tomorrow."

But the next day was equally quiet. Equally long. Equally unnerving. Tracy did smile at them once, but then, remembering, she wiped the smile off her face with the back of her hand. Another time, Jason came barreling toward them on his skateboard as though he were going to run them down. They stood their ground, but at the last second, he veered off in another direction.

Toward the end of the day, Mr. Donovan called an assembly.

The dam broke. Words rushed out — all

of them splashing against Nora and Jennifer.

"I hope he really gives it to you."

"Cedar Groves'll never have another chance."

"You deserve whatever you get."

Nora and Jennifer didn't hear any of it. It was all drowned out by the flood of accusations inside their own heads. Yes, they had done their best, but what good was that when their best just wasn't good enough?

Mr. Donovan strode out onto the stage.

Jennifer grabbed Nora's hand.

He checked the mike and cleared his throat.

The two girls exchanged agonized glances.

"As you all know," the man began, "Cedar Groves Junior High was selected as one of five schools statewide for the honor of Model Junior High School."

Nora and Jennifer slid down in their seats.

"Being a nominee is an honor in itself," the principal continued, "All the finalists are excellent schools. Top schools! To be selected as the best among the best, a school must have that extra something." Mr. Donovan looked around at his silent audience. He seemed confused, as if he were not getting the response he had expected. He cleared his throat again.

"Get on with it," Jason murmured.

"Hit us with the bad news," Tommy seconded.

The principal held up a piece of paper. "I have here" — he fished his reading glasses out of his breast pocket — "a letter — *the* letter! — from the selection committee." He slipped on the half-glasses and began to read.

The first paragraphs said what Mr. Donovan had already said about the importance of being a finalist.

People yawned and shifted uncomfortably in their seats. Some closed their eyes. Most closed their ears.

Nora squeezed Jennifer's hand. In return, Jennifer pulled back the corners of her mouth and rolled her eyes. This was agony!

" 'The winning school,' " Mr. Donovan read, " 'is to be commended for its open and free atmosphere which allows for individual differences and promotes learning. We further appreciate the lack of any attempt by faculty and student body alike, to appear perfect. There is no doubt that the winning school is *A good place to grow.*' "

Nora snapped to attention. She had heard that phrase before! CEDAR GROVES — A GOOD PLACE TO GROW. It was on one of the posters. "We won," she mumbled. "We won!" She was on her feet, murmuring, "We won! We won!"

Jennifer pulled her back into her seat, but she sprang up shouting "WE WON! "We won! We won!"

The hushed audience fixed its attention on Mr. Donovan. Beaming, he nodded at Nora and raised his arms over his head. "Cedar Groves Junior High is Model School of the Year!" he confirmed.

That brought the rest of the crowd to its feet. People cheered and clapped and whistled and stamped their feet. The girls jumped up and down and hugged one another. The boys jumped up and down and hugged one another.

After several minutes, Mr. Donovan held up his hands for silence. "There is responsibility attached to this honor," he told the restless group. "Next week, we will host visitors from all over the state. We will need your help and cooperation. There are sign-up sheets in each home-room. Please stop by before you leave school and volunteer. We want everyone to know that Cedar Groves has spirit!" Giving one last victory sign, he strode off the stage.

Nora sat down beside Jennifer. "Now watch them change their tune," she said, fully expecting their classmates to beat a path to them, anxious to heap them with congratulations.

Instead, everyone beat a path to the door. They couldn't seem to get out of the auditorium fast enough in their rush to get to their homerooms.

"I guess winning is gratitude enough," Nora said as the last person left the room.

Sighing heavily, Jennifer heaved herself out of her chair, "I'm not sure we deserve thanks," she said.

Ambling up the aisle beside her friend, Nora replied, "We won, at least."

"Right," Jennifer said without enthusiasm. She knew she should be excited, but, for some unknown reason, she felt depressed.

In room 332, there were long lines in front of each bulletin board.

"What's going on?" Nora asked Denise.

"We're signing up for next week like Mr. Donovan said," she answered.

"You mean all these people are volunteering?" Jennifer asked incredulously.

"Every single person in the whole homeroom," Tracy said. "Isn't it awesome?"

Nora stepped behind Jason. "We'd better get in line, Jen, or there won't be any jobs left."

Jason flashed them a lopsided grin. "That's the whole idea," he said. Then, seeing the hurt looks on their faces, he added, "Just kidding. Hey, maybe we really couldn't have done it without you."

Lucy motioned the two girls to take places in front of her, but Nora and Jen exchanged glances and by unspoken agreement declined and stayed at the back of the line. Somehow it felt safer — even though here and there, people were beginning to smile at them again.

"There must be a positive side to all this," Jennifer said on the way home, "but I don't have a clue what it is."

"We won. That's positive."

"Yeah, well," Jennifer responded glumly.

Nora walked along in silence. If optimistic Jennifer couldn't see the silver lining, it could be gold and she herself would miss it. "Well," she said, making a valiant effort, "at least we don't have a job to worry about."

"That's true," Jennifer conceded. She'd welcome the rest. She had enough to do with her other projects. "Did you see who signed up? I mean there were people in that line who have never signed up for anything!"

"That's it, Jen!" Nora exclaimed. "The positive side! If it wasn't for us, the same old people would've signed up."

Jennifer brightened.

"You know what else?" Nora went on. "If we hadn't done what we did — if we hadn't tried to make everything so perfect, everyone would have walked around *pretending* to be perfect for the judges, and we probably would have lost."

Jennifer smiled. "You're right!" she said. "We provided the atmosphere, like Jeff said."

"Right." She chuckled. "And who else could have done it so well? Our best is pretty good, Jen. You have to admit that. Sure, we made some mistakes, but so did everybody else."

Jennifer brushed that aside. "No one's perfect."

Linking arms with Jennifer, Nora laughed. "To look at some of us, who'd know?"

When the eighth-graders stay overnight in an old inn, scary happenings make them wonder . . . is a ghost *a guest in the inn, too? Read Junior High #13,* WHO'S HAUNTING THE EIGHTH GRADE?